I0539791

MAN *from the* S K Y

a novella

DANNY WYNN

BACON PRESS BOOKS
WASHINGTON, DC
2014

Published in the United States by Bacon Press Books, Washington, DC
www.baconpressbooks.com

Editor and Copyeditor: Lorraine Fico-White
www.magnificomanuscripts.com

Cover Design: Alan Pranke
www.amp13.com

Book Layout and Design: Lorie DeWorken
www.mindthemargins.com

Cover Photo: Dana Wynn

Author Photo: Dana Wynn

ISBN: 978-0-9888779-9-3

Library of Congress Control Number: 2014930501

PRINTED IN THE UNITED STATES OF AMERICA

For Toby and Billie

TABLE *of* CONTENTS

MAN *from the* SKY

"[H]e had the amazing feeling, both upsetting and liberating, that . . .

he was about to take his life into his own hands for the first time."

Pascal Mercier, *Night Train to Lisbon*

CHAPTER
one

The small propeller plane, white with blue markings, burst noisily over the craggy mountaintop, much lower than seemed right to Jaime. He'd heard a muffled engine noise before, but the acoustics of the mountains made it seem remote. He was out on his morning hike high in the Tramuntanas, the glorious Mediterranean sparkling off to his right, far below. He was seventy-three years old, and the steep mountain range on the western coast of the island had been his true home since birth.

It was a sunny day in late May, the island in full bloom, wildflowers abundant, bright colors and variety beyond anything seen during the hot, dry summer months. The temperature was just right. There wasn't another person in sight. No houses, either, though there were a few not far below, including his own, blocked from view by the fall of the land. He was using a walking stick— hickory, unadorned—which helped considerably with his creaky old knees, especially on the downslopes. And he wore a beat-up Panama hat. He had mixed feelings about hats for the sun— they provided shade, of course, but held in a fair amount of heat as well. His medication was working decently. He was moving well, not too much, not too little. The trail he was on led all the way to Fornabufar, a village about a dozen kilometers down the coast, but his goal that morning was much more modest—about halfway up to the ridgetop and back down.

Shortly after the plane came into sight, to Jaime's surprise, the door on the near side opened and a man climbed out onto one of the struts. And after what looked like a false start, jumped. A white parachute popped open almost immediately, and the swaying figure floated downward toward somewhere above Jaime on the mountainside. The plane continued to fly northwest toward the big shimmering sea, gradually losing altitude.

It was a very odd thing to see. A man dropping out of the sky, high in the Mallorcan mountains. Jaime considered the phenomenon for several moments and got nowhere. He watched the plane move away, its noise already faint in the big open sky, then hurried up the path to find the man. He wore hiking sandals with toe coverings, definitely necessary, as without them his shuffling gait had a tendency to result in painfully stubbed, sometimes bloodied, toes.

As he trekked uphill, he turned and looked back a few times. The third time, he saw the plane, by then far away and quite low, veer gradually to the left, then wobble and dip, and plunge abruptly into the sea, raising a distant white splash. Quickly, the surface of the water smoothed over, and there was nothing to see other than the vast expanse of dark blue and a few small boats a long way from where the plane went down. He stood there stunned. The plane was gone. He could hardly believe the whole thing, happening right in front of him, in what was more or less an extension of his backyard.

———

Stefan was bunching up his parachute when below him he saw a man with a walking stick trudge out from behind a large rock formation, on what looked like a trail. The man stopped there, about sixty meters away, breathing hard and looking up at Stefan. He raised his hand in greeting.

Stefan lifted his hand in response, hoping this encounter would mean help rather than trouble. His right foot had landed on a small rock and his ankle folded partway under. He stood with some weight on the foot, but it was sharply painful, and he wondered how much of a problem it was going to be.

The man walked up the grassy slope between them, dotted

with small vivid-red wildflowers. The brim of his hat shaded his face, but he seemed to be elderly. He was wearing khaki cargo shorts and sandals with thick soles made of some lightweight synthetic material.

He stopped about fifteen meters away and called out, *"Buenos días."*

Stefan turned to face him more directly, and winced as he put too much weight on his injured ankle. "Hullo," he said.

The man glanced at the navy blue gym bag lying in the grass a couple of meters from Stefan, then said, *"Te vi echarte del avión. Qué pasa? Estás bien?"*

"I don't speak Spanish," said Stefan.

"I saw you jump from the plane. Are you okay? What happened?" The man's English had an American accent with a Spanish tinge.

"Christ," said Stefan. "The pilot passed out at the controls. I couldn't rouse him, didn't know what to do. We were still over land, headed out to sea." The words came rushing out. He was talking as much to himself as to the man.

"I was scared shitless," he went on. "Wasn't sure I'd even know how to work the parachute. Or if there was enough height."

———

Jaime knit his brow as he absorbed the fact that the parachutist seemed to have just abandoned another man to die in a plane crash. He understood wanting to parachute while still over land, of course, but even so . . . There must have been something the man could have done, though Jaime couldn't think what it was, not if the pilot was really out, beyond reviving. It must have been a crazy situation.

The man looked about forty-three, forty-four, six feet tall, wiry. Dark wavy hair swept back from angular features.

"The plane went down in the sea," said Jaime. "Did you see it?"

"Yeah," the man said with a grim expression.

Jaime waited for him to say more. He was aware of a vague inner excitement. His life in the Mallorcan countryside was quite uneventful. The strange event, though horrible, was definitely an interesting break in his routine.

"Are you hurt?" he asked.

"Yeah, my ankle. But I don't think it's too bad." The man gingerly put some weight on his right leg. He was dressed in a wrinkled, white, button-down shirt, black jeans, and loafers. "This is Mallorca, right?"

Jaime nodded. He had lots of questions: What was the guy doing on the plane? Who was the pilot? What exactly happened? But he decided not to ask for the moment.

"My house is below, not that far. Let's see if we can get you down there, and we can figure out what you want to do from there."

The man agreed.

He insisted on carrying the gym bag despite his injury. Jaime carried the parachute, which was bulky and turned out to have some weight. It prevented him from effectively using his walking stick.

"By the way, my name's Jaime," he said as they started down.

"Mine's Stefan. Thanks for your help."

Jaime kept up an intermittent patter as they walked. His meds were beginning to wear off, and he had a few moments of rigidness, which caused him to step haltingly, as if his joints needed oiling, but he was pretty sure he managed to cover it up. Stefan said little and seemed to concentrate on managing the terrain with his injured limb. Two fighter jets zoomed overhead from the military installation down the coast. Jaime and Stefan watched as they flew in a matter of moments to roughly where the plane went down in the sea, swoop low over the water twice, then head back south.

"Well, I guess the authorities are aware of a plane going down," said Jaime.

"Yeah," Stefan said in a flat tone.

"We should probably call somebody anyway. Let them know you got out. Tell them whatever you know about the plane, the pilot. That we saw it go down."

"I'd rather not," said Stefan with a certain firmness. "It won't change anything, won't do any good."

Why doesn't he want anyone contacted? Jaime wondered. *Is there something shady going on? Is this guy dangerous? Should I be concerned? He doesn't give off a dangerous vibe. Just the opposite, in fact. Though people can definitely fool you.*

They approached the back of Jaime's renovated *finca*, with its orchard of gnarled olive trees on the left and spectacular view of the Mediterranean spread out in front, far below. The house was about two-thirds of the way up the mountain, the highest house on one of the dead-end roads branching up from the winding corniche. Stefan took it all in without comment. Some untended goats wandered nearby, bells on their necks ringing clearly in the silence of the mountains. One of them bleated loudly.

Jaime found he was glad that Elena, his housekeeper, wasn't coming that day. He wanted to get more of a sense of the situation without an audience, even a very unobtrusive one.

———————

Stefan showered in Jaime's guest quarters, where Jaime had put him to freshen up. The guest quarters had a separate entrance and consisted of a spacious bedroom with its own small terrace and bathroom.

"Come over to the main house whenever you're ready," Jaime had said.

Stefan toweled himself off roughly and thought, *What the fuck do I do now? What's going to happen? Are they even going to know what happened? Are they going to hear about the crash? Do they have ways of finding these things out? Will divers go down to the wreck? Is the cargo still intact? Is that even possible? Doesn't seem likely. If they do go down, one thing they're not going to find is two bodies, though between the crash and the sea, there's not a lot they could make of that.*

Maybe they'll never know what happened. They're not exactly going to broadcast they lost a plane. Though with corruption, who knows what they can find out these days? With all the technology . . .

I don't know. I don't know anything. And that's just the start of the questions. The real question is how they'll react if I go back to Paris and tell them what happened? It wasn't my fault. I didn't screw them. Their pilot passed out, had a heart attack or something. What was I supposed to do? I can't fly a goddamn plane. We were over land almost definitely for the last time. I had to make a decision.

It's not my fault, but how will they see it? I'm nobody to them, someone they were using for the first time, on Felix's say-so. Are they going to say fine, let's give it another go? Or fine, on your way, no problem?

I have no idea. I don't know how they think. And I don't want to find out.

———————

As Jaime led him into the living room, he noticed Stefan's limp was more pronounced. Jaime directed him to the couch, facing the view, and handed him a pillow, saying, "Here, put your leg up. It will keep the swelling down."

Stefan followed the suggestion, as Jaime went into the kitchen and brought out a tray of coffee, orange juice, water, and toast. And a bottle of aspirin. Stefan took three tablets and swallowed them with water. Jaime poured their coffees and sat down.

Stefan sipped his juice and looked around the room and out the glass-paned French doors at the view. Jaime noticed flecks of white in Stefan's dark hair. There were small hollows under his cheekbones, and his nose was slightly hooked. He had a dashing look, handsome in an eastern European way. There was something appealing about him. Between that and his looks, it struck Jaime that a good share of the nice things in life had probably come his way.

"So," Jaime said, "your plane went down and the pilot died. Are you sure we shouldn't be contacting someone?"

"I'd really rather not," Stefan said with a chagrined look. "Like I said, it won't do any good. No good at all."

And it might do some bad? thought Jaime. *For you?*

The silence crackled between them.

Eventually, Stefan shifted uncomfortably and said, "Nice house. You live here year round?"

"Yes. I grew up in the village just down the road. Teix. Left a few times, but always came back."

"You could've done worse."

Jaime nodded.

"Palma's the city here, right?"

"Yes."

The jingle of wind chimes drifted in from outside.

"So, what happened?" Jaime asked.

Stefan shook his head. "I haven't been able to work out a good story to tell you yet."

Jaime registered that and didn't press the point. "Well, then, where are you from?" he asked.

"Paris. But I don't think I'm going to be able to go back there." Stefan shook his head again and reached over to massage his ankle.

"What's your accent?"

"South African."

Jaime sipped his coffee, then said "Do you want to use the phone? Do you want me to help you get somewhere? A doctor for your ankle?"

Stefan shook his head again, closed his eyes, and kneaded the back of his neck. He seemed worn out, drained.

On impulse, Jaime said, "Why don't you rest here for a few hours, and then you can figure out what you want to do?"

Stefan didn't react right away, staring off sightlessly. Eventually he said, "Thanks, I'll take you up on that. It's very kind of you." The genteel expression seemed slightly out of character.

Jaime stood and picked up the tray. "I'll be in my study." He nodded to a room off the living room with the same expansive view. "Let me know if you need anything."

CHAPTER
two

Jaime sat at his desk and ruminated. His chair was positioned so his view was out a large window filled with sky and sea, but the panorama might as well have been a blank wall that afternoon for all it registered on him.

It seemed pretty clear Stefan was involved in something illegal, and the most likely thing was smuggling drugs from North Africa over to the continent. Massive amounts of contraband were smuggled north across the

Mediterranean almost every day. Tax-free cigarettes alone were a multi-hundred million dollar business.

He was aware he was taking more than a passing interest in Stefan. He should probably just help him on his way as quickly as possible, especially given the likely criminal activity. Maybe he should even call the police on his own, over Stefan's objection. But he felt an internal resistance to making trouble for him. He seemed okay. Besides, it was an interesting situation, and Jaime suffered from something akin to a deep malaise.

His dispiritedness had developed over a lifetime. His father had been an American archaeologist who came to the island in late middle age and unearthed some caves containing artifacts and wall drawings, all of which turned out to be highly significant in certain academic circles. The discovery formed the basis for the remainder of his life's work. He married a Mallorcan woman, a moderately successful painter, and settled down with her in a house in Teix. Jaime was their only child. His parents used the traditional pronunciation of his name, HY-may, but in his adolescence, he switched to the more progressive JAY-mee and stuck with it.

His early childhood was idyllic in some ways—he ran around the local countryside, much of which was still in its primeval state, swam in the sea, dove off the big rocks, mixed with the artsy expatriate families that came and went. But his parents never took much interest in him, absorbed in their work and much preferring adult intellectual company. And not too many years into his young life, his parents were overwhelmed by his mother becoming sick. He was raised by Marta, the Mallorcan woman who worked for his family. He loved her more than his parents in an everyday sense, and maybe overall as well.

From the age of eight, for the next four years, he watched his mother become increasingly unable to move properly. It was confusing and frightening for him to see her hands and limbs shake for long intervals, see her freeze mid-movement, prompting him to hold his breath sometimes until she moved again, see and hear her struggle to form words, and eventually struggle to perform basic movements. In the end, she was almost completely paralyzed by the disease, unable to speak at all.

Jaime learned later that each case of Parkinson's was different, and his mother's was a fast-progressing one. Her death from complications came only seven years after onset; Jaime hadn't noticed her less severe symptoms during the first few years of her illness or couldn't remember. After her death, his father withdrew even further into his work.

His parents were now both buried in the village cemetery, next to the church. He'd mourned Marta's death more than those of his parents.

Eventually, Jaime had ventured out into the world, not very well prepared, going to Cornell University, his father's alma mater, in freezing upstate New York, which as far as he was concerned was like going to Mars. Not only were the winters beyond brutal, but he was also a provincial foreigner and didn't fit in well. Occasionally, he felt the lure of the infamous deep gorges that sliced through the magnificent campus; the pedestrian bridges over the chasms were part of his daily routine.

Later, he lived in New York City, working for a small book publisher in a desolate part of Tribeca. But his life there hadn't taken hold, and he kept drifting back to Mallorca, sometimes for extended periods, and returning to New York. It didn't help that he wasn't confident with women. He was tall and skinny, not bad looking, though his hair thinned early. But confidence either comes from within or doesn't come at all.

He knew what it was like to urgently want to kiss a woman and know it would not be welcome.

Money was never a concern, thanks largely to his deceased father, who had his mother's family to thank for that. Jaime didn't live extravagantly, right up to the present. He inherited his parents' house in Teix, to which he had no great attachment. At one point, he took a flat in London, but life there proved even more impenetrable than New York. He gradually gave up on making a life in the outside world. It was as if there was something missing in him, something needed to coalesce with the great swirl of mankind. He eventually sold his parents' house and bought the *finca* outside town where he now lived, to which he did quickly form a great attachment. From the first time he'd seen it on a hike, uninhabited, in dilapidated condition, he knew he wanted it to be his home. After persuading the three estranged siblings who co-owned it, two of whom didn't live in the area, to agree to a price, and bribing a local official to get permission for certain renovations, he was able to make it happen.

His turn with the disease eventually arrived and started to wrap its life-sucking tentacles around him. He'd had symptoms now for six years, and so far it hadn't progressed nearly as fast as with his mother. With regular doses of synthetic dopamine, he was still able to function acceptably, but the medication had started to cause dyskinesia—uncontrolled herky-jerky movements, twisting and tensing. Incapacitation loomed ominously in front of him, sometimes flooding him with fear. He was resolved to not go as far down the road of misery as his mother, no matter what.

Over the last fifteen years or so, Jaime had struggled to be content with his life, to be comfortable with the solitude, the quiet, the boredom. And for a while, he'd succeeded to an extent. He was part of the village community in a low-key way, enjoyed the company of a few people there. Occasionally drove to far parts of the large island, and spent a night or two in a small hotel. Ventured into Palma sometimes, the only city on the island, with a few hundred thousand denizens. He gardened, walked in the mountains, read a lot. Had the olives from his orchard harvested and pressed each year, producing an excellent oil, most of which he sold to a posh local hotel.

But more and more, he found himself wanting the day to be over, wanting it to be time to slip into the unconsciousness of sleep. And in early evenings, his ennui could reach a pitch that was frantic.

He hadn't actually been off the island in three years. At this point, going elsewhere for a change seemed an even lonelier prospect than life on the island. In a way, he felt trapped on the beauteous isle, trapped *by* it. Yet, at the same time, it was his home.

Often he felt in a sharp stinging way that he'd missed out on life, that he hadn't really lived, had somehow been denied the full experience. He tried to reconcile himself to this, accept it as the way things had turned out. But he couldn't entirely shake the feeling, couldn't manage to lock it away in a drawer or a closet.

Late in the afternoon, Stefan knocked on the partly open door to Jaime's study and entered. "Well, I guess I'm going to go into Palma," he said. "Is it possible to get a taxi to take me there from here?"

"Yes, I can arrange a taxi. The drive is a bit less than an hour, and it should cost you about forty euros. I'll call one for you."

However, after a few minutes on the phone in the other room, Jaime came back in and said with an apologetic smile, "I'm afraid there's only two taxis in Teix, and they're both in Palma right now and booked for the evening."

Stefan smiled, mildly amused. "How else can I get there?"

"Well, there's a bus from Teix and a train from Muleta, about twenty minutes from here. But neither of them has any trips scheduled late in the day." He paused. "Why don't you stay here tonight, and I can run you into Palma in the morning? Or you can get a taxi then if you'd rather."

"No, I couldn't, thanks. There must be some place in the village where I can get a room for the night. Can I trouble you for a ride into the village?"

"Don't be silly. You're injured. And moving to a hotel just for tonight will be more bother than it's worth. I insist you stay."

Stefan shifted uncomfortably where he stood. Grimaced as he

put weight on his right foot. He could see Jaime had a point—
it would be a hassle, and it was just for one night. Besides, it
appealed to Stefan that, standing there in Jaime's remote villa, he'd
pretty much disappeared from the face of the earth. Except for
Jaime, there wasn't a soul on the planet who had even a glimmer
of where he was.

"Okay, thanks," he said. "If you would, please arrange a taxi
for around nine thirty in the morning."

"Excellent," said Jaime. "When the sun drops a bit lower, I'm
going to do some gardening. After I clean up from that, we'll have
dinner. Feel free to read any of the books in the house, watch TV,
though the reception is pretty bad, or listen to music. You can
use the computer if you want—there's a guest account—but it
works on a dial-up basis since this area hasn't been wired yet for
faster methods, so using it can be downright painful."

———————

As Jaime pruned plants in the late afternoon sun, he thought of
Elena, who would arrive in the morning. He'd tell her that a friend
from London had unexpectedly visited and stayed the night.
Plausible enough, though he had few visitors.

Elena had worked for Jaime for a half-dozen years, and he
modestly lusted after her. She was middle-aged, nicely plump
with a generous bosom and a pleasant face. From what he knew,
she lived in the outskirts of Muleta with two brothers. She drove
a rusty, light green Vespa to and from Jaime's house, bringing him
fresh *ensaimadas* in the mornings, which he hadn't requested

but liked her bringing, even if the rich breakfast bread sometimes went uneaten. Jaime understood there had been a husband at one point, but no more, and Elena had a grown daughter living over in Palma.

On the next road over from Jaime's that came up from the corniche, there was a run-down old mansion where the aging local abbot lived. Attached to the residence was a massive outdoor cage containing a number of peacocks that screeched relentlessly whenever a car drove by or anyone approached. The abbot's longtime housekeeper had a teenage daughter, whose provenance was murky, and it had long been rumored that he was the father. That was the kind of relationship Jaime fondly imagined having with Elena—her continuing to take care of his house and him, but taking on a more intimate role in his life, as well. Who knew, maybe it could be a good thing for both of them.

CHAPTER
three

Stefan stood outside on the terrace and sipped a gin and tonic that Jaime had made for him. Jaime was inside engaged in dinner preparations. Stefan felt as if he was on holiday, which seemed ridiculous given the situation.

Jaime's natural instinct was to treat his surprise visitor as an invited guest, so dinner had taken on a social feel, despite the weird circumstances. With his own gin and tonic in hand, Jaime walked outside and joined Stefan. They wordlessly watched the molten sun descend into the immense darkening sea, a river of reflected gold running up the middle. Purple bougainvillea spilled down from a small second-floor balcony on their right, and in front of them to the left stood a large outdoor sculpture, abstract and made of steel.

Dinner consisted of thinly sliced cured meats, a simple pasta, bread, salad, and wine. Stefan thought they would eat at the rustic kitchen table, but Jaime set a table in the living room just inside the middle set of French doors leading to the terrace, open to the night air.

Stefan looked at the finely set table with real silverware and cloth napkins. It flashed through his mind, not for the first time, that Jaime might be gay, but his instincts said no.

The dinner conversation unfolded awkwardly, but Jaime's non-pushy, non-threatening manner relaxed Stefan and gradually he opened up considerably.

It turned out he was forty-nine. "I've bounced around a fair bit," he said, "mostly in London. Worked as a concierge in a few different hotels, as a maître d' in some nice restaurants."

It struck Jaime that Stefan did have a stylish, aristocratic look that a certain type of establishment would like to project.

"I'm good at taking care of things," Stefan went on, "a skill a surprising number of people don't have. And I'm good at dealing with people, especially upscale types. They like to feel they're dealing with someone from their own world, even when that's obviously not the case."

He gestured toward the table and said, "By the way, the food is very good."

Jaime nodded. "Yes, it's simple but we have excellent ingredients around here." Then he asked, "Wife? Girlfriend?"

"No, not for a while. I've had my share of romances, but . . . In the jobs I've had, you get a lot of wealthy older women making their interest clear. Not that there haven't been others, younger women, but for some reason older women seem to sense something about me. Being with a rich older woman makes you wonder about yourself sometimes. What you're doing, where you're headed. And now I'm older, myself." He gave a rueful grin.

Stefan was conscious he was being more forthcoming than usual. But somehow, being in this remote spot with a total stranger, and the bizarreness of how he got there, brought out the urge in him to reveal. He realized he hadn't talked to anyone like this in a long time. He had lots of acquaintances, but few, if any, real friends. It was a relief to speak freely up here on the mountainside in the darkness, to this older man. An expression came to him from the country he grew up in—the back of beyond. That's what this place felt like.

Stefan could tell Jaime was worldly to a fair extent, but he also seemed like he might be a recluse with related eccentricities. Stefan noticed Jaime's hand shaking and wondered what that was about. Jaime slipped the hand under the table.

"I helped a client once," Stefan said, dipping a piece of bread in a dish of olive oil, "a guy staying at the hotel where I was working, very successful. I helped him make a bunch of tricky arrangements, and he took a liking to me. Nothing out of order. He was impressed with me and arranged for me to get a position in New York repping a new line of beauty products. Marketing and selling." He smiled at the memory. "I had no experience, but in a way, that was what I'd been doing all my life—marketing and selling myself. So, I lived in New York for a few years. Unfortunately, the line never quite took off. It was competing for shelf space in the big chain chemists, and that's extremely tough space to get, especially in the States. But I did have a fantastic time in New York." He smiled again. "That is one stupendous town."

Jaime noted that Stefan's conversation was a curious mixture of casual and educated speech.

He mentioned he'd also had stints as an assistant photographer, going on chic fashion shoots in various locales, exposing him to more milieus that were a long way from his roots. Occasionally, when he was particularly short on funds, he worked as a clerk at a stock photo agency in London, where there was a guy he knew from the nightlife.

"I guess I've always been something of a hustler," he added as an afterthought.

Jaime, in turn, told Stefan about some of his forays off the island, including a few long stretches spent neither in school nor working. During those periods, the bulk of his time was spent reading books and going to the cinema.

"Back then," he said, "big cities had lots of art houses playing off-the-beaten-track films and well-known ones that deserved another screening. Some films really need to be watched on a big screen. Like *Days of Heaven.* Every scene in that was filmed in late afternoon light. Every shot is like a painting."

Stefan indicated he wasn't familiar with it, but Jaime's allusion to the special visuals piqued his interest. He wondered what a film lit entirely that way looked like.

"In a way," Jaime said, "reading books and watching films are the blessing and curse of the modern age, when a fair number of people have escaped at least the complete tyranny of fundamental necessities. It might have been better when people didn't have the luxury of looking for meaning in their lives."

Toward the end of the meal, Jaime brought out some cheeses to eat with the red wine left in the bottle. He said, "You don't look particularly South African, at least not of Dutch or English ancestry."

"No, I come from generations of Serbs. Serbs get a bad rap these days, deservedly so, of course. Even after the war, they didn't stop behaving badly. In Serbia now, the government and the mafia are almost the same thing, literally. There was a time, though, when Serbia was part of old Europe with culture and tradition. My surname is Mihailovich, an old name there. My great-grandfather was a general who led resistance fighters in the southern mountains against the Nazis. Unfortunately, America and England chose to back Tito and the communist resistance, and my family pretty much lost everything, including a lot of lives.

"Anyway, shortly after I was born, my parents managed to get out of Tito's new Yugoslavia and move to South Africa where there was a Serbian émigré community. My mother told me my father thought he'd have opportunities there, but if he did, we never knew. He disappeared shortly after we arrived. My mother and I never heard from him again." He fiddled with the cheese knife.

"She was a very beautiful woman, my mother. As far back as I can remember, there were always men around in one way or another who helped with the bills, sometimes a lot. I even went to private school in Switzerland for a couple of years, though that came to a sudden halt when the man of the time had a heart attack. I came back down to earth fast."

They lingered at the table, looking out at the night. The light from a quarter moon had turned a patch of sea into silver; the running lights of a boat floated along in the distance.

"So, how do you wind up sitting here this evening?" Jaime chanced a probing question.

Stefan didn't say anything for a good fifteen seconds or so.

Jaime waited.

Stefan then said, in a voice that sounded almost as if he was talking to himself, "Life gets less forgiving as you get older. For one thing, your looks don't work for you the way they once did. Remember the line in the song, 'Once I was a young man, and all I had to do was smile.'" He grinned.

He became lost in thought for several moments, rubbed the side of his face harshly; he had a few days' growth of salt and pepper whiskers. "I was in London," he went on. "Wallet extremely thin, as usual. A French guy I knew told me about a new restaurant opening in Paris that was looking for experienced people with some polish. I speak French pretty well, and it turned out to be a plus that I was foreign. I was a bit *exotique* for them. And I got a job as one of their maître d's.

"I moved to Paris, but the restaurant struggled, and after a year, closed. I was basically stranded in Paris with almost no money, living in a tiny room with a shared bathroom across the hall. Not an ideal situation for a forty-nine-year-old guy.

"One day, I ran into a customer from the restaurant, a regular from its few popular months, a guy named Felix. A classic *boulevardier*, if you know the type. He had this thin pencil mustache and hair that was always oiled, perfectly combed. I told him about my situation. He took down my contact info and got in touch the next day. We met for a drink, and he made me a proposition."

This time, Stefan stopped talking for an inordinate length of time, and Jaime wasn't sure he was going to continue.

He resumed in a distant tone. "The proposition was this—go to a city called Melilla on the northern coast of Morocco. Oddly enough, it's actually part of Spain, some quirk of history. There I was supposed go to a certain brothel and meet the woman who was the bookkeeper. She'd put me on a small plane with a pilot and a load of cocaine, and we'd fly to a place in the countryside in the south of France, away from the coast. It turned out to be near a town called Carcassonne, over toward Spain. Someone would meet us there with a car, and I'd drive the car to Paris with the coke in concealed compartments. Leave it in a garage there. For that, I'd be paid five thousand euros. Not a lot of money for some people, but for me a fortune, a chance to get back on my feet. I was literally close to being homeless at the time, didn't even have the cash to get back to London where I might've been able to scrounge a bit."

He bowed his head and plunged his fingers into his thick hair, digging them into his scalp. Then looked up and said, "It turns out life isn't over when you're down to your last thirteen euros. That's when it really gets serious."

Stefan knew it was dumb to be telling Jaime all this. But his situation was so strange and dire, he felt a strong compulsion to talk about it. As at the outset of the dinner conversation, the house's location, Jaime, and the odd circumstances all tended to make Stefan feel temporarily cut off from the outside world, strangely safe.

"Anyway, everything went smoothly until the pilot—who turned out to be this surly Mexican with almost no English—slumped sideways in his seat on the plane. I shook him, slapped him. He was breathing but wasn't coming out of it, whatever it was.

"Now, here I am, and I have no idea what to do. I don't even know if the Paris guys are going to know what happened."

Stefan filled Jaime in on his speculations from earlier in the day, then concluded, "The Paris guys, I don't know how they'll react. I didn't screw them. What was I supposed to do? Maybe I should've dumped the rest of the cargo out before I jumped. Yeah, I probably should've. But that would've taken time and composure, and I didn't have either.

"There's nothing really holding me to Paris. Should I go back? Doesn't feel like it. Not at all."

They sat in silence for a while. It was a lot to absorb, even for Stefan.

Jaime rose and went into the kitchen to get a bottle of brandy, the fine Juan Carlos Primero he liked. While he was in there, he quickly swallowed a batch of pills. He came back into the living room with the bottle and two snifters, sat down, and poured.

"What about money?" he asked.

"Felix gave me a bunch of cash for expenses, and there's still a fair amount left. And I have my passport. So, I can function to some extent. My knapsack was already stuffed in the gym bag, along with my toilet kit and a change of underwear. I don't have a cell phone—it was turned off a couple of weeks ago for nonpayment. Felix gave me a phone card to use if I ran into a problem."

"Well," Jaime said, inhaling the fumes from his cognac, not taking a sip yet, "I'm far from the right person to give advice on something like this, but I can see how you might be reluctant to go back to Paris. Whoever Felix works for could well take the position that in their line of work there are no excuses, only results. Or they might think you're lying to them and trying to rip them off, hiding their drugs somewhere. Or maybe they don't want to use you again, and you know too much. Or maybe they're just superstitious and think you're bad luck.

"It's not definite they'll react in any of those ways, but the problem is you don't know, and the only way you're going to find out is to put yourself in harm's way. And then you won't be able to avoid the harm if they aren't the 'honor among thieves' type of criminals, so to speak."

Stefan nodded. "And," he said with his clipped accent, "like I said, what the hell do I have to go back to Paris for? To take a chance of getting killed or who knows what? Nothing. Nothing at all."

It wasn't until later that night when Jaime was alone in his bedroom that he realized Stefan's gym bag might very well contain a large amount of cocaine. Stefan's phrase "the rest of the cargo" echoed in his head. While Stefan may not have been speaking precisely, the wording must have meant something—most likely that there was some cargo that didn't go down with the plane.

It was stupid of me not to think of it sooner, he thought. *I wonder how this other cargo fits into Stefan's thinking.*

If it's true, having a serious amount of illegal drugs in the house is not a good thing. Not a good thing at all.

———————

Jaime had trouble falling asleep that night. He got up and went out onto his balcony. The sky had clouded over, and it was very dark. His mind drifted from the stimulation of the day to the general sorry state of his life.

Often, when he woke in the mornings, the day stretched out endlessly in front of him. He would feel acutely anxious about how long the day was going to be —in recent years, his temporal experience of twenty-four hours could stretch to as much as fifty or sixty hours—and about whether he could get through the waking hours without his deep-seated boredom becoming a silent scream. And that was just one day. After that, there was another and another. Though, thankfully in some ways, the end of such unpleasantness was now in sight, still off in the distance, but in sight.

On most mornings, lying in bed after he woke, he reached for the book on his bedside table to pick up where he'd left off the night before, or maybe a page or two back, though usually he had to shuffle to the bathroom and relieve himself first. For most of his life, reading in bed first thing in the day, even briefly, had felt like one of life's great small pleasures. Lately, however, reaching for the book held less and less appeal. It seemed empty of purpose and meaning. *Why should I read?* he frequently thought. *What's the point?*

For decades, he'd read almost every day for hours on end— morning, noon, and night. It varied. Reading had long been an immense source of comfort. These days, though, his constant plowing through one volume after another seemed to be little more than just occupying his brain with the words and thoughts of others, strangers. As ingenious and inspired as some of the works were, they were other people's stories. What about his own life, his own stories? The few he had seemed trivial and long ago.

It frightened him to think that maybe one of his last refuges was close to being used up.

After he rose for the day, he usually went into the kitchen and had a simple breakfast—maybe cereal, some fruit, coffee. Then he might go out for his morning constitutional, though he'd been skipping that of late sometimes, which he knew wasn't good. Later in the day, he might garden, maybe drive into the village, though there often wasn't any particular reason, and he might well not talk to anyone there.

Intertwined with his stultifying routine was his loneliness.

That most pitiful of sadnesses. Sometimes, he felt so lonely it ached in his very core. He got used to it to an extent, but people never really get used to loneliness. He didn't have any real friendships and hadn't for a long time, wasn't completely sure he'd ever had any. The only relatives he was aware of who might still be alive were some cousins he'd met once as a child, and he had no idea where they might be at this point. He'd never had a truly in-depth romance with a woman, never lived with a woman, at least not so that he or she had given up their abode. The women he'd spent time with had seemed like lost souls themselves, and with each of them it had felt like two solitary people not really connecting.

He sometimes wondered what it was like to truly open up to another person, to have someone genuinely know you.

Sometimes he went days without talking to anybody other than Elena. He felt like he was gradually being erased. As if his lack of meaningful human contact and lack of function was causing him to disappear, parts of him already transparent, holes that other people could see through. He was afraid that one day he'd look in a mirror and wouldn't see anyone.

It wasn't that he was without appeal or interest as a person. He was just profoundly withdrawn and to a large extent had given up.

Even if he were inclined to try again to make some changes in his life—get involved in more activities, put himself in more situations where he would interact with people—he was running out of time. His disease was picking up speed. He had a limited amount of decent quality life left, a limited amount of future in which he'd still be able to manage adequately.

It seemed odd, but lately, for some reason, he'd been trying to remember what it was he'd been out for in life when he was young, what he'd dreamed of being when he grew up. And he'd been drawing a blank. He must have had some thoughts along those lines but couldn't manage to summon them up. Strange, but there it was. It occurred to him that maybe that was one of the things at the root of his considerable inadequacies—he'd had no dreams. Could that really be?

One thing he knew for sure—this was no way to live. It wasn't really living.

CHAPTER
four

In the fog of first wakefulness the next morning, Jaime was conscious of feeling disconcerted. Initially, he assumed it was having a complete stranger in his guest quarters, and as he thought about it, a criminal. Plus, very possibly, a serious quantity of illicit narcotics. But in the shower, with the water pouring over his head, he realized it was more than just those things. When Stefan rode away in the taxi, that would be the end of it, that would be the last he'd see of him. The flurry of excitement would be over; he wouldn't find out what happened, wouldn't find out the ending to the story. His regular life would resume.

While he shaved, Jaime thought about driving with drugs in his car and decided it was a low risk. Mallorcan police weren't usually a strong presence, and he'd never been pulled over in all his years there. He'd long driven like the elderly man he now was—stayed within the speed limits, obeyed the other traffic laws.

In some ways, he couldn't believe he was even thinking about this. It was so much out of character, at least the character he'd manifested for most of his life. In another way, though, he understood what was going on inside him, saw it with clarity and accepted it. In a person's life, a man doesn't drop out of the sky every day, literally or more importantly, figuratively. It almost definitely wasn't going to happen again in his life. He felt a rush of pride as he sensed himself about to give in to some recklessness.

Over juice and coffee, he said to Stefan, "Listen, I've been meaning to drive over to Palma myself. There's a hard-to-find light bulb I need to get for my desk lamp." Lame but true. "So I can drive you over this morning. Help you find a hotel."

Stefan looked at him for a few moments, then said, "You sure?"

"Absolutely."

"Okay." Stefan shrugged. "Thanks."

Jaime cancelled the taxi, and within a half hour, they were on the road in Jaime's Hyundai station wagon. It was another beautiful spring day.

On the winding coast road into Teix, well above the sea, they saw a helicopter flying by with a grand piano hanging beneath it.

"What the hell is that?" asked Stefan.

Jaime laughed. "The BBC is making a film about Chopin living near here. It must be for that."

As they approached Teix, there was a road sign indicating the town limit.

"So that's how they spell it," said Stefan. "I'd never have guessed it from you saying 'tesh'."

As they passed through town, Stefan looked around with interest. The village was exceptionally well-preserved and beautifully situated on the slopes of a horseshoe-like indentation in the mountains, descending into a valley leading to the sea. Virtually every house and building was built of a pale salmon-colored stone, which went perfectly with the rugged mountain backdrop of dry browns and greens and pink-tinged grays. The aura of the place, its tranquility, made Stefan wish he could stay there and forget about everything, not just the immediate crisis but the overall dilemma of his life as well.

They continued along the road from Teix to Fornabufar, the next village down the coast. Jaime refrained from pointing out any of the route's majestic features, letting Stefan take it all in. To Jaime's way of thinking, it would be a rare person who wasn't struck by the visuals of the drive. At some points, the cliffs on one side plunged precipitously at least a hundred meters to the sea, and on the other side, the cliffs rose with equal steepness. Along the way, pine forest was interspersed with terraced olive orchards and massive rock formations.

At Fornabufar, they turned inland and cut through the mountains down a roller-coaster stretch of descending s-curves, to the vast plains below stretching over the rest of the island. Jaime's left arm began to ache from constant involuntary tensing on the steering wheel. He took his left hand off the wheel and shook it vigorously. Peripherally, he saw Stefan glance at him.

The flatness of the rest of the island surprised Stefan, and he turned and looked back at the wall of mountains.

About halfway to Palma, Jaime said, "So, what are you going to do?"

"I have no idea."

"It occurred to me that your gym bag might contain a substantial amount of cocaine?"

Stefan didn't respond.

"Maybe a small portion of what was on the plane?"

"Yeah," Stefan said reluctantly. At this point, he gave up on resisting the urge to confide in Jaime. He wasn't a very good criminal.

"What are you going to do with it?" asked Jaime

Stefan shrugged, which seemed to be a form of expression he favored. "Try to sell it," he said

"How are you going to go about that?"

"I don't know. Go to some bars, clubs. Talk to people. Maybe some strip clubs—there's always dodgy people hanging around in them. Maybe try to score a little something to see what's what. I'm probably not going to be able to unload it all in one go, though it's not like I'm going to be holding out for a top price."

"Very risky. Hit or miss. And there could be a lot of misses before you get a hit. You're not going to want a lot of people knowing what you're up to."

Stefan nodded, acknowledging the truth in all that.

They drove past massive olive orchards, and the stone walls along the road were in better shape than those in the mountains.

A thought had formed in Jaime's mind over the course of the trip, and when it came into focus, he deliberately pushed himself to come out with it before he had a chance to fully think it through. "I know a couple of guys who might be able to help you out. Not dealers or anything like that, but they might know people, might have some suggestions."

Stefan looked over at him and said, "You don't want to get involved in this." He found he liked Jaime, even if his level of assistance was a bit strange, and of course he was very grateful to him.

"I won't get involved. I'll just introduce you, see if they might be able to help you out."

"Why?"

"I don't know. You seem like a decent guy. Got yourself into a bad situation. Seems like you could use some help. I suppose I have some objections to drugs, but not really strong ones, and this is Spain where people are going to do their party drugs no matter what." Jaime was well aware, as were most Spaniards, that over the past couple of decades, the Spanish had become major consumers of drugs, especially in connection with their ultra-late nightlife. "Besides, it's not like this is going to be a regular thing, right? This is a one-time ticket to a new life for you."

They approached the outskirts of the city.

"Who are these guys?" asked Stefan in a tone devoid of expression.

"One works as a captain on a yacht over in Portal Nous. The other guy works as a private cook back in Teix."

They crossed over the highway that circled the back of the city. Stefan said, "How would we go about it?"

"I could call Johnny over in Portal Nous right now and see if he's around. We could drive over and talk to him."

Stefan was silent to a point where Jaime wasn't sure he was going to respond. He was off by himself somewhere. Then he said in a fatalistic tone, "Okay, let's do it."

———————

Jaime pulled over to the side of the road and called Johnny on his cell. It went to voicemail. "I'm almost certain he's in port," said Jaime. "He called me about something last week and said he'd be around. We could just drive over there and see if we can find him?"

Stefan nodded okay.

Portal Nous was about a dozen kilometers west of Palma, which they covered quickly on the highway. It was a pretty town—quiet, tree-lined streets, modern, well-maintained villas, manicured grounds—set in the hills just above the southern coast of the island.

They drove down a hill to a modern marina and parked the

car. The harbor-front buildings, rather than being the usual mix of traditional structures, consisted of a posh strip mall containing restaurants, boutiques, and realtors. There were only a few customers strolling around; it was a little after ten in the morning.

Stefan sensed that the clientele for the most part were people who dressed ultra-conventionally, in ways that clearly labeled them as affluent and successful. *Ralph Lauren country,* he thought.

They walked out on a long, wide, wooden dock—Stefan limped—past one uber-luxurious yacht after another. There was activity on a number of them as crew members, many in uniform, performed maintenance tasks and provisioned their crafts. Jaime and Stefan came to an extra sleek vessel named *Sabena.* Jaime unfastened the small chain across the gangway, and they walked up onto the deck.

"Johnny," he called out, and after a lengthy wait, a lanky crew-cut man in his fifties emerged, dressed in navy blue shorts, a white polo shirt, and canvas boat shoes.

"Jaime, what brings you to the harbor of the nouveau riche?" he said in a raspy voice with an English accent. It sounded like his vocal chords were slightly damaged.

"To see your good self, young Saunders."

Johnny looked skeptical but didn't say anything.

"Johnny," said Jaime, "I'd like to introduce you to Stefan, a friend of mine who dropped in unexpectedly."

Johnny nodded at Stefan coolly. Stefan reciprocated with a slight smile.

"Anyone else on board?" asked Jaime.

"No, but I've got a couple of crew coming back from the chandler's soon." His accent was of a well-heeled variety.

"In that case, can you take a little walk with us?"

Johnny gave a puzzled frown. "Well," he said facetiously, "I was just getting into a particularly gripping volume of Nietzsche."

"Please?" Jaime asked patiently.

Johnny gestured to Jaime and Stefan to lead the way.

Jaime led them to the end of the dock, where they stood, Jaime in the middle, facing the massive stone seawall that protected the harbor. The big wall was gray and wet, with a wide opening for boats to come and go, and seaweed sloshed around at its waterline. Jaime felt his head start to bob and weave involuntarily and tried to stop it, hoping neither of them noticed.

"Johnny, this is a strange one," he said. "To cut straight to the chase, Stefan is in possession of a large amount of cocaine he wants to sell. And it occurred to me that you might have some idea of how to go about doing that here in the Balearics. There'd be money in it for you, of course." Jaime hadn't discussed this last part with Stefan, but assumed it was okay from what he'd said earlier.

Johnny looked at Jaime as if he'd suddenly grown a second head. Then he looked at Stefan, seeming to take a new measure of him.

"Jaime, what the fuck are you on about? This isn't your thing. Not at all."

"I'm just trying to help Stefan out. He's in a tough spot."

"My gut reaction is to tell you to get the hell out of here, and don't come back until you've reentered your body and returned to being your doddering old self." Johnny paused. "Who the hell is this Stefan guy, anyway?"

Stefan stood next to Jaime, listening. Gave no reaction.

"And how did he come upon this big batch of Charlie? How come he doesn't know what to do with it himself? Not that I'm discussing any of this with you 'cause I'm not. I just want to bring to your attention a few of the things you'll want to focus on before you completely fuck up your golden years."

Jaime was pretty sure Johnny wasn't aware of his disease.

Stefan didn't say anything, leaving the difficult conversation to Jaime.

Jaime stared out to sea and considered whether it was worth it to go on, explain more to Johnny, or just drop it. He decided to proceed and filled Johnny in about Stefan dropping out of the sky and the failed smuggling effort. He concluded, saying, "You know what it is to be in trouble. I was hoping because of the family friendship, you might be willing to help out, at least share your thoughts, whatever you know about these things. I know you take the boat over to Ibiza pretty often. I thought you might know of people over there who'd be interested."

Johnny stared at Jaime and said, "Let me talk to you for a minute," cocking his head to the right.

The two of them walked several steps away.

"Why are you doing this?" said Johnny in a loud whisper. "How do you know this guy? You don't need the money. What gives?"

"I don't know," Jaime said quietly. "It seems crazy, I know. But I feel like . . . like I want to help him do this thing. It feels . . . *real,* like nothing I've ever done before. I don't know. Maybe I'm just trying to breathe some life into my out-to-pasture existence, feel the blood flowing in my veins."

Johnny snorted. "I don't even know what all that means. But it could turn out very badly. Very badly indeed."

The waves slapped against the dock at their feet. The seagulls screeched.

Johnny finally said, "I'm not your guy. I might be able to put you in touch with people. I don't know. You don't need to go to Ibiza, I know that. There's plenty going on here. Between the Brits in Magaluf and the Germans in Arenal. Plus the clubs in Palma. How much does Icarus here have?"

Jaime waved Stefan over and asked.

"Eight keys," he said. "Uncut, I assume. At most, stepped on lightly."

"Christ," muttered Johnny. "Whole lotta blow. What's it worth?"

"A key of pure should be worth about thirty thousand. But I don't expect to be able to get that much. I'll sell it at a bargain price to unload it all, but it'll probably be hard to sell it all in one shot."

"Yeah, well, it's not like you got any costs of goods sold," Johnny said sarcastically. "Whatever you get will be pure profit. I bet if someone offered you a hundred thousand for the whole lot right now, you'd take it." Stefan's personal appeal wasn't working on Johnny.

Stefan utilized his favored form of expression——he shrugged.

"Let me have a think," said Johnny. "I don't know if I could help even if I wanted."

"You understand, of course," said Jaime, "you have to be very selective in who you talk to about this? And no discussion of how the stuff got here."

Johnny nodded grimly. "Give me a couple of days."

———

"How do you know him?" Stefan asked as they drove back toward Palma on the two-lane coast road, this one much closer to the sea. They passed through a number of villages-turned-suburbs.

"My father was friends with his parents. They used to come to Teix every summer. They were big in the London art world, had a successful gallery there for a long time. Johnny was just a kid then, not a particularly pleasant one, as I recall. He wound up in the British Army—had a lot of discipline problems growing up—and he went AWOL one time too many. To avoid prison time, his family shipped him out here. I helped him get on his feet. He's never been back to the UK, though I'm pretty sure he could at this point if he wanted."

They entered Palma from the west and drove along the wide seafront boulevard, a low concrete divider down the middle, palm trees lining the way and the immense harbor on their right. A stunning number of boats, thousands—big, very big, small, almost all of them white—docked at one marina after another. A forest of masts and antennas. They drove past enormous piers with towering cranes rising above them, freighters alongside. Jumbo ferries were at dock as well. On the city side of the curving boulevard were mostly nondescript modern buildings, streets and avenues leading like spokes into the city. A cathedral rose prominently in front of them, farther along the enormous bay. Not a beautiful city, but bustling and fairly clean. With sunshine and sea, too.

After about a kilometer, Jaime pulled into a parking area next to a modern-style café between the boulevard and the water. They bought coffees at the counter and sat at an outside table in the warm sunshine.

"So, what now?" asked Jaime.

"I suppose I find myself a hotel."

"And explore your other options?"

"I don't know. I guess so. It doesn't sound like I should count on Johnny. What do you think?"

"I'm not sure." Jaime sipped his coffee. "Where are you going to keep your goods while you're here?"

"I don't know. Leaving it in the hotel room when I'm out doesn't seem like a great idea. I could put a lock on the gym bag to keep nosy maids out, but . . . hotel rooms get ripped off. And it's probably not smart to carry the stuff around with me. Maybe there are lockers in a bus or train station, like in the American movies. Though you wonder how often they clear those things out. I think terrorism may have done away with them, anyway."

"That sounds about right," Jaime said. "There really isn't a good approach. What's more, you'll have to show your passport to check into a hotel, which means you'll have to use your real name." He paused for a few moments to let Stefan absorb that. "I've got a suggestion. Why don't you come back with me and stay at the house a bit longer?"

Stefan frowned and looked at him hard, then said with an edge in his voice, "Is it the money? Is that why you're doing this? If it is, that's fine, 'cause I'm more than happy to share with anybody who can help. But it's *really* not smart of you to get involved."

"If I said it's the money, would that make it easier for you to accept my help? To tell the truth, I'm not entirely sure why I'm trying to help. I know it doesn't make sense. But I also know that unless you're willing to use your real name to check into a hotel and leave your goods in a hotel room while you're out, you don't have a lot of good options."

"You realize that if the police find the stuff at your house, you'll be in deep shit. This is *not* a minor thing. And if some unsavory types were to find out the stuff was at your house . . . I assume Johnny's trustworthy?"

"He's okay. A bit abrasive, but I trust him."

They listened as the cathedral bells rang twelve times.

"So, what do you think?" asked Jaime.

Stefan turned away, looked in the direction of a strip of grass where a couple was laying in the shade of a tree. He didn't want to check into a hotel under his real name even more than he didn't want to leave the drugs in a hotel room. Jaime's offer was a blessing, as much as he wanted to operate on his own. He hadn't been looking forward to floundering in the dark.

He said quietly, almost as if to himself, "It does seem like the best option. It'd mean exploring things here in Palma would be a lot less convenient, though maybe that's a good thing." *Trying to plug into the local drug scene through bar chitchat,* he thought, *could easily turn into a disaster. Even if it worked, I'd probably be counting on some low-level guy to hook me up with someone who could handle weight.* He shook his head. "I'll accept your generous offer for the time being," he went on. "But I want to say again, so you hear me loud and clear, you're being completely stupid and crazy."

They headed off to buy Jaime's light bulb.

CHAPTER
five

"Jaime," exclaimed frumpy Birgitta in her overly enthusiastic way. "Where have you been keeping yourself? I feel like I haven't seen you in months."

"Birgitta, how nice to see you. Let me introduce Stefan, a friend of mine from London."

It was the evening of the day Jaime had taken Stefan to meet Johnny. Jaime and Stefan sat drinking beer at an outdoor table at Davall, the bar-café at the heart of social life in Teix.

Davall was an institution of sorts, though an exceedingly plain one. Situated on an elevated terrace about five meters above the village main street, on the uphill side, it was not much more than a cracked, uneven cement surface with an iron railing along the edge, and some rickety mismatched tables and chairs. There was a small stone building at the back housing a heavily scarred wooden bar. The terrace was shored up on the street side by a tall hand-built stone wall running along the narrow sidewalk, the same type of support wall used for the farming terraces scattered over the nearby mountainsides. Built into the wall, alongside it, was a narrow set of worn stone steps leading up to the bar.

Most of the terrace had shade either from trees or an overhead trellis covered with reed mats and leafy vines. From certain vantage points, the views looked out over the terra-cotta village rooftops cascading downward, to the towering mountains across the valley, textured with dusty browns, greens, and pinkish-grays. On summer nights, the people who gathered at Davall could include all ages from newborns to old folks, an eccentric international celebrity or two, and almost always a few characters.

"Well," said Birgitta, "a guest from the outside world. That's nice."

Jaime found Birgitta mildly annoying and a bit sad, though harmless enough. She was one of the village's year-round expat residents. She was German, of some indeterminate middle age, an affluent modern-day hippie. She could have been from northern California but for her guttural accent. She fancied herself a painter and regularly sent signals to Jaime that she thought they could enjoyably relieve one another's loneliness. But she had free-floating anxiety in her and a tendency to spread it.

Her paintings, mostly landscapes, were amateurish—crude daubs of Mediterranean color—but she'd managed to get a local shop to display a few. Over the years, there had been a couple of sales. Jaime imagined the buyers as foreigners with rustic second homes on the island, who went for the bohemian look and thought a primitive local painting might contribute.

She hovered by their table nattering until Jaime invited her to sit down with them. As she talked, Jaime only half-listened to her and thought back over the day's events.

When Jaime and Stefan had returned to the house that afternoon, Jaime introduced Stefan to Elena and said, "He's a friend from England. He's going to stay in the guest quarters for a few days, maybe a bit longer."

Elena smiled at Stefan with her eyes lowered, then said to Jaime with a serious expression, "*La policía* were here. They asked whether anyone here had seen *una avioneta* flying in the area yesterday. I told them I wasn't here yesterday and that you weren't *en casa en este momento. La policía* said they'd come back."

Teix had no police of its own, so they must have been from Muleta or even Palma.

Jaime and Stefan exchanged a look. There was no reason yet to think the police were focused on a drug angle, though small planes probably tended to raise that possibility. Jaime had only been moderately nervous up to this point, but this new development increased his jitters palpably. He wondered how stupid he was being.

As evening approached, Jaime found Stefan out on the terrace sitting under the pergola, reading a book of Jaime's, *Saint Jack*. Jaime said, "Why don't we go into Teix this evening? People around here tend to notice strangers, and it might be best for you to act like a normal visitor to the island. Besides, you may as well get a sense of the village while you're here. It's a special place."

Stefan didn't answer right away. His thinking had been that the safe, disciplined approach would be to leave the house as little as possible and keep his interaction with other people to a minimum. He realized, though, there was going to be some waiting involved in his efforts to turn the coke into cash, and there might be something to what Jaime said about acting like an ordinary visitor.

"Jaime, you're not even listening to me," Birgitta said.

He smiled and said, "Of course I am."

Slightly exasperated, she turned to Stefan and asked, "So, how do you know our resident hermit?"

"I met him at our local pub back when he was living in London. We became friendly, and when I decided to come out to Mallorca for holiday, I looked him up." This was the story Jaime and he had agreed on.

Davall began to fill up. They were joined at their table by Chantal, a half-Indonesian, half-Dutch woman, who had a small boutique in the village where she sold a variety of things—clothing, jewelry, statuettes, carvings, ceramics, candles—which she brought back from annual trips to Thailand, Bali, and similar places. She was thirty-eight years old and very independent. Six feet tall in flat sandals, surprising to some people, given her Asian features. Extremely attractive. During the five years she'd lived in Teix, Jaime had seen many men come on to her without success, though he suspected she occasionally succumbed discreetly. He and she had become friendly, without any romantic overtones. Jaime knew there was no fool like an old fool and easily suppressed any impulse to flirt with her. They had a rapport, enjoyed running into one another and talking. They were both moody and seemed to understand each other's moods. She had a sadness in her that never seemed to completely lift. And he, of course, had his own murky inner currents.

Stefan and Chantal quickly became immersed in conversation, and Jaime was left to people-watch, listening vaguely to Birgitta blather on while he sipped his beer. He was both amused and mildly put off by a group of hipper-than-thou teens at the next table, which included the daughter of an aging British rock star. He figured it must be some kind of school holiday across Europe for these kids to be out in force this early in the season.

Later in the evening, after they were all a bit tipsy, Antonio came in, the private cook Jaime had mentioned to Stefan as possibly being able to help. He also worked as a caterer in the area. Argentinian. In recent years, a lot of Argentines had come to the island to work and live.

Jaime pointed him out to Stefan across the terrace where he was standing with some other people, and added quietly that he didn't think they should broach anything with him just yet. They might hear from Johnny fairly quickly, and it probably wasn't a good idea to let anybody in Teix know about the endeavor until they had to.

While Stefan was up to get more drinks, Chantal turned to Jaime and said, "Your friend Stefan is quite charming. Somehow, I wouldn't have put the two of you together."

"Well, you know me," he said blithely, trying to gloss over her remark. "I'm full of surprises."

Antonio sat with them at one point. He seemed to take a quick liking to Stefan as well. Before long, he discreetly conveyed to Stefan that he had some blow, and Stefan was welcome to join him for a line.

Stefan didn't usually do coke—didn't particularly enjoy it—but the opportunity to interact with Antonio in the needed context seemed too good to pass up. He slipped off with him into Davall's kitchen, unused at night, and standing there among the hanging pots and pans and clean metal surfaces, did a couple of healthy bumps. Antonio clapped him on the shoulder and said to let him know if he wanted more.

During the course of the evening, Jaime watched as various people responded to Stefan's magnetism. He wondered what it was like to go through life like that, having charisma. He'd always been intrigued by the curious phenomenon—people being manifestly drawn to you for no reason other than some intangible allure you were blessed with, having nothing to do with any of your more specific attributes. *Must be nice,* Jaime thought. He had always been someone easy to miss in a crowd.

Jaime and Stefan stood outside on Jaime's terrace on the mountainside watching jagged slashes of lightning skitter in the distance across the night sky. A whipcrack of thunder sounded soon after, followed by a deep rumble. The rain was still a ways off, and there was an odd absence of wind where they stood—the literal calm before the storm. When they'd gotten back from Davall, Jaime guided them outside to watch the light show. Stefan was still buzzing slightly from the bumps with Antonio, which he hadn't mentioned to Jaime.

"No observations about the universe, please," Jaime said.

Stefan looked at him questioningly.

"People who come out here at night are usually moved to make profound remarks. I think I lack a sense of the profound. Profundity is lost on me."

"Well, you needn't worry about me," said Stefan. "I'm a simple guy."

They stood in silence a few moments.

"How's the ankle?" asked Jaime.

"Not bad. Getting better. It'll be okay in a few days."

"What'll you do when you get the money? Where'll you go?"

"Oh, probably London, maybe New York. Try to pick up my life. Hope nobody's looking for me."

"I'd go to Argentina," said Jamie wistfully. "Buenos Aires. I've always wanted to go there. People say they have the most beautiful women in the world there, not that that's ever been so relevant to me. Promiscuous, too, I'm told, if that appeals." The lights in the house went off for a moment and then back on. "I guess it's one of those places people think of going to disappear."

"Yeah, if you're a Nazi," said Stefan.

Jaime winced and smiled at the same time. "It's supposed to be a really great place, whatever your reasons for moving there. Supposed to be beautiful, good weather. Fairly sophisticated, inexpensive to live. And yes, a good place to hide."

"That's quite a picture you paint there. It might not live up to expectations."

Jaime ignored the remark, saying, "No, that's the place to go." His voice sounded as if his mind was in a faraway place.

"You know, man," said Stefan, "you've got a great life here. I've picked up that you don't think so. You seem to think your life came up short. But everyone's life comes up short in some ways. You learn to live with how things turn out. And your life turned out okay. You may not think so, but your life is good."

Jaime didn't say anything.

After a while, Stefan asked, "Why do you shake?"

"I have Parkinson's."

"I've heard of it, but don't really know what it is."

"An incurable brain disease," Jaime said in a monotone, all feeling removed from his voice. "People are born with a certain amount of brain cells governing their movement, more than they need, and those cells gradually die off in the course of their life. For people with Parkinson's, those cells die at a much faster pace than normal, and eventually there's not enough left to control your movement properly. There's no cure, nothing you can do to stop the cells from dying too fast. You can only control the symptoms, or try to. I take large doses of synthetic dopamine, which substitutes for the natural dopamine my dead brain cells are supposed to be making, but over time you need more and more, and eventually the synthetic dopamine causes uncontrolled movements of its own."

"How are doing with it?" asked Stefan. "How are you holding up?"

"*Comme ci, comme ça.* My mother was severely crippled by the disease and died. It's not strictly hereditary, but they think people who get it have a genetic predisposition, which gets triggered by something in the environment that makes the disease blossom, if a disease can be said to blossom. They haven't been able to figure out what the environmental trigger is yet. Someone's going to win the Nobel Prize one of these years for figuring that out.

"Recently," he went on in a clinical way, "my meds have started to be much less effective, which is why you see me shaking and probably have noticed some other things, too. I'm already taking very high doses. The illness has started to become extremely unpleasant for me.

"On top of all that, another symptom is depression, in case the rest wasn't enough."

When he was done, he stood there for several moments, the hidden emotion that was stirred up inside him subsiding. "Goodnight. I'll see you in the morning." He went inside, leaving Stefan standing in the dark.

————————

The next day, Stefan borrowed Jaime's Honda 50cc, which Jaime didn't use anymore, and rode into the village by himself. He bought a

Tribune at a small food shop and went to Davall to have some coffee. As he read the paper and sipped the rousing Columbian brew——the irony wasn't lost on him——he felt like he almost belonged.

Antonio emerged at the top of the stairs leading to the elevated terrace, and when he saw Stefan, came over and sat down. He was a stocky guy, with longish, straight, dark hair and a ready smile. He wore jeans, sneakers, and a red-and-blue Barcelona Football tee shirt. The night before, Stefan had sensed that, beneath his affability, he was continuously alert and observing. Stefan also picked up that he had a strong desire to be liked, though was relaxed about it.

As they talked, Antonio told Stefan about his widespread travels in South America when he was younger. "A lot of it was by motorcycle," he said. "Like Che when he first went traveling. Che's a hero to a lot of young Argentines.

"When I was sixteen, I lived in Punta del Este, working at a beach resort. The whole region was an enormous nonstop party. Later on, I went up north to Bahia. A trendy village called Trancoso—— helicopters from Sao Paolo and Rio dropping out of the sky into the third world, all dirt roads. I worked at a fancy spa there."

Later in the conversation, he described how he spent six months working at a shamanic retreat in the Peruvian jungle, where people came from all over the world to take ayahuasca, the powerful natural hallucinogen used for the purpose of searching the soul. "Some of them, I don't think they could find their souls," he said.

Stefan sipped his coffee and listened. Waited until what seemed like a good moment, then said, "Would you by any chance be interested in acquiring more of what you shared with me last night? Very high quality. Good price."

Antonio looked surprised and discomfited for a few moments, but it passed. "It's possible," he said cautiously. "How much are we talking about? What price?"

Stefan assumed Antonio was a small dealer, not handling weight, though he might well know people. He wasn't focusing on a big score right then and didn't want to scare Antonio away. He just wanted a cash infusion and to get a feel for the local drug scene.

"Say, half a key for five thousand euros. Very high quality." He aimed for what he thought Antonio might be able to swing. "It's a great price, as I'm sure you realize."

Antonio looked at him, gauging, trying to intuit. Stefan waited.

"Maybe," Antonio said. "I might know somebody . . . I'd need a sample."

Stefan nodded.

On his way back to the villa, he decided, without pushing himself to figure out exactly why, not to tell Jaime yet about his approach to Antonio.

The police showed up at Jaime's house around noon, two of them, one middle-aged, overweight, the other young and stone-faced. Jaime came outside to talk with them. Stefan had gone down to the rocks for a swim.

The older cop asked the questions in gruff Spanish. "Did you see *una avioneta* fly over *hace dos días*? Go down in *el mar*?"

"No."

"We had a *declaración* that somebody may have parachuted from *un avión*. Have you seen anybody *no familiar* in the area?"

"No."

"Does anyone else *residir* here with you?"

"No. I have *un invitado* visiting from London. He's in the village right now, but we were together *todo el día* on *el día* you're asking about."

"*Su nombre.*'"

"Charlie Hall," Jaime said. His face had lost some expressiveness in the last few months due to his ailment, and he wasn't sure whether this made him seem more or less credible.

The middle-aged cop looked around, seeming vaguely dissatisfied, but it could have just been his usual manner. Jaime felt a slight undercurrent of menace but thought he might be imagining it. The police thanked him perfunctorily and left.

The encounter drove home to Jaime that he was now fully involved in a serious illegal activity. It made him feel queasy and prompted him to revisit his stupidity level. But there was still no specific reason to think the police were focused on drugs.

When Jaime drove into the village later in the day, the police were sitting in their car parked at the bottom of his road, the older one in the passenger seat talking on a cell phone. The other one, who Jaime had noticed was stocky and solid-looking, eyed him as he drove by.

Jaime arranged a dinner with Stefan and Chantal. He was pleased Chantal and Stefan had hit it off. In a silly way, he thought of both of them as his protégés.

He decided on El Viejo, the popular village tapas restaurant, as he wanted a casual lively setting. Plus the food there was superb. Another village institution. Housed in an old stone barn with extra-high ceilings, massive rough-hewn beams, and a stone floor worn smooth. Big haunches of cured meats hanging from hooks along one stretch of wall, glass display cases full of mouth-watering offerings, pitchers of sangria, bottles of wine, and a wildly eclectic array of paintings on the walls, all lent to the convivial rural atmosphere.

As Jaime and Stefan drove to the restaurant, Jaime found himself in a full-fledged good mood, something he hadn't felt in a long time. Soon after they arrived and settled on stools at the bar, Chantal walked in looking more beautiful than he'd ever seen. She was statuesque, wearing a colorful flowing summer dress and delicate leather sandals; her Dutch/Indonesian features were tastefully made up. People looked her way as the three of them were shown to their table. Stefan looked dashing with his Slavic features, swept-back hair, freshly laundered, white, button-down shirt, and black jeans.

A renowned woman photographer from New York sat with a large contingent at the next table. It was rumored she was gradually going blind, one of life's cruel twists if true.

Partway through dinner, Birgitta came in with a boisterous group of people, and they were seated across the room. She barely nodded at them and didn't come over to say hello, very out of character for her. Jaime suspected she was put out at not being included in their group; three could so readily be four. It was easy to be disdainful of Birgitta, but Jaime knew he was not so different than her, though winding up living year-round in Teix was more a natural outcome for him. And he was probably better suited to the isolation of the long off-season.

After dinner, Stefan and Chantal wanted to stop by Davall for a nightcap. Jaime excused himself, feeling it was the right time for him to bow out.

On his way home, when he came to the bottom of his road, a police car was parked in the dark, the glow of cigarettes inside. He couldn't tell if it was the same police.

The barometric pressure seemed to suddenly shift.

———————

"I have a daughter," Chantal said to Stefan, glasses of red wine on the table in front of them.

It was a weeknight and late; Davall was quiet, with only about a dozen customers. A well-known playwright sat at a table with a couple of male companions, impressively intoxicated. It struck Stefan that for a small remote village, there were a surprising number of people with some claim to celebrity.

"How old is she?" Stefan asked Chantal.

"Twenty."

He raised his eyebrows.

"I had her when I was eighteen." She paused. "I left her with her father in Amsterdam. I was young, with an all-consuming ego and a need to experience life that was overwhelming. I didn't see how I could do that and take care of her at the same time. So I left and moved to Paris. Got a job as a chorus girl at the Moulin Rouge. I trained as a dancer for many years when I was young. Worked there for six months. Then got a series of jobs as a runway model. I was one of Azzedine Alaia's favorites for a while. I danced in a cabaret show in Monte Carlo one summer. Jack Nicholson was staying in a villa on Cap Martin, and I went out with a friend of his. Jack called me 'pretty face' all summer. I don't think he ever knew my name.

"I traveled to lots of places. A famous Brazilian artist decided I was his muse and painted me several times, mostly nudes. I wish I had one of them now. I'm told they're worth a lot of money."

Chantal was interrupted by an American woman stopping to say hello and how much she loved the sarong she'd bought in Chantal's shop.

"So I got to have the life I wanted," she resumed. "But I left my daughter behind. And never really got over that, as I'd known I wouldn't, deep down. Never forgave myself. Not that I should have. It was a monstrous thing to do, egotistical beyond belief. Disgusting. I got to a point where I could hardly believe I'd done it, that I'd had it in me, the capacity to leave my baby. My baby girl . . . What kind of woman does that?"

Stefan was torn between wanting to convey to her it wasn't that bad and knowing she would recognize that as bullshit. Being real won out. It struck him that she would reject absolution if it was offered.

"I went back to Amsterdam fairly often and spent time with her," she went on. "Her name is Zoe. I tried to have a relationship with her. Leaving her each time was very painful. The fact I was able to do it over and over again shows just how selfish and hard I can be. Now she's grown up and starting her own adult life. She's never fully forgiven me, which I completely accept. She's coming here next month to spend part of the summer with me." A nervous eager expression came over her face.

"I'm sure she'll have a great time," Stefan said, feeling the urge to ease her bad feelings about herself and not quite sure what else to say. He found her authentic and perceptive. She had a quiet elegance about her.

"We were all young once and did foolish things," he went on. "I got married when I was twenty-one. To an English woman six years older than me. A wonderful, beautiful woman. Much better than I deserved. I could never have appreciated her properly at the time. I didn't even really stop running around for more than a few weeks. Cruising the nightlife, 'chasing girlies,' 'watching the whites of my eyes turn red.' And one day, she was gone. To an older guy, more mature, more established. He recognized her for the gem she was and treated her like it. It rocked my world. I never saw it coming, had no idea it was a foregone conclusion from the start.

"But I was young and frivolous, and life went on. Before I knew it, I was onto the next stage of my life. And the next. Somehow, the demise of my marriage caused my rootless nature to fully kick in. From then on, life became something that more or less just happened to me. I went with the current. I was lucky. Life without moorings suited me well. I had lots of good times, hung out with lots of interesting people, in lots of interesting places and situations. Some of the people were actually all right. It all worked up to a point where things began to run out of steam, started changing. It seemed like the life I'd led up till then just wasn't as available to me anymore. It was as if it was fading, or I was fading, like a photograph left out exposed to the sunlight."

Later, they walked through the sleeping village to her flat at the other end of town, closer to Palma. She comfortably took his arm. They turned into a steep uphill alley, with sloping stone steps every four or five feet; they took their time until they came to the highest part of the village. Stefan was out of breath; he laughed and said, "You're not breathing hard at all."

Her flat was on the second floor of what had once been a traditional village house. Inside, her place was stylish with a warm pleasing feel, decorated in a colorful Moroccan way with a few Far Eastern touches. Outside her large sitting room window, rose the towering mountain at the back of the village, a pure mass of darkness in the night. She said the mountain was supposed to contain a special ore giving off emanations that stimulated people's creativity, a notion Stefan found quite appealing. On a sideboard was a framed photo of a pretty girl with reddish-brown hair—her daughter, Zoe.

As their clothes gradually came off, Stefan was stunned by her body. Its full magnificence had been hidden in the loose-flowing clothing she usually wore. She had long legs, a full shapely bottom, and a waist that narrowed distinctly. Her breasts were medium-sized and plump, beautifully natural, with protruding pinkish-brown nipples. Her skin was a gorgeous honey tone. She looked incredible for any age but truly extraordinary for thirty-eight. He was glad for his own narrow hips and still lean, wiry body, so he could have some confidence in his own nakedness. He was physically enthralled by her. And in a few other ways as well.

As they made love with him above her, lost in a deep pleasing rhythm, at one point he lifted himself off her, arching his back, slowing his movement. He gazed down at the unique soul-stirring beauty of her face and felt he could never tire of looking at it. She opened her eyes and held his stare. He looked into her dark green irises encircling her deep black pupils and had the sensation of falling into a wondrous place.

When he woke in the morning, she was next to him still asleep, her long dark hair covering all but a few traces of her face, spread out over the pale green pillowcase. He thought of the innocent child she must have once been. He smiled.

CHAPTER
seven

Antonio sat by himself on the ratty couch in the small apartment he shared with three of his compatriots, in the bottom part of the village where the sun never quite managed to shine. Not at any point in the day. It was an exceedingly plain apartment, three small rooms with some basic furniture; the only thing on the white walls was a slightly torn poster of Maradona, the great Argentine footballer from another era.

It was late morning. Two of his roommates were out at their jobs at one of the local hotels, and the third one was sleeping in one of the shared bedrooms, as he usually was at that hour; he worked the late shift at Davall as a barback.

Antonio took out the torn folded piece of magazine paper that Stefan had brought to him containing the sample. He noted that the content was crystallized into small chunks and had a pinkish tinge, both of which traits he took as favorable signs. He tipped the *yeyo* onto the messy glass surface of the coffee table; there were empty cans and stains on it, a dirty ashtray, and even a pair of underwear. He used the back of his cell phone to crush the chunks into powder, rolled up a ten-euro note, placed one end of the note in the opening of his left nostril and the other over the white powder. Inhaled sharply and sat back.

The neighbor's rooster crowed loudly several times. Sometimes Antonio would crow back and spur the bird on to a more lengthy session.

Ay dios, he thought. *This shit is amazing.*

He was filled with euphoria, mostly from the narcotic, but some from the thought of having such a fine product to sell. He felt like getting up and doing something. He almost woke his roommate to give him some. He felt like a powerful jet plane smoothly lifting off and heading for the sky.

He couldn't believe it. He'd never had coke like this.

———————

The next morning, Antonio and Stefan stood by themselves in

Davall's empty kitchen, this time with dirty dishes on one of the stainless steel counters and in the sink.

As Antonio handed Stefan twenty-five hundred creased euros, he said, "Man, your stuff is like pharmaceutical cocaine. Like the Merck product the rock stars used to talk about. Not that I've ever had any, but this is how I've always imagined it— smooth, strong, lasting, not too speedy, stuff that can pump you up to march through the Bolivian mountains all day long."

Stefan handed him a doubled-up plastic baggie with a generous estimate of a quarter key in it.

Antonio had scrambled and quickly gotten together as much cash as he could on short notice, tapping the Argentine network. He planned to cut the coke to triple the quantity. It would still be more potent than anything else on the island. The price was a steal, which he wondered about, but not too hard. No point looking a gift horse in the mouth. He was going to make what for him would be a small fortune. He felt great and hadn't even done any of the super-fine *yeyo* that morning.

―――――――

The same day, Jaime followed up with Johnny by phone, who said, "No, I haven't come up with anything yet. But there's a few possibilities. I need a bit more time."

Jaime was a little surprised that Johnny seemed to actually be trying. After he got off the phone, Jaime wondered for the umpteenth time whether he'd made a mistake helping Stefan out. Of course, he'd made a mistake. No question about it. But people knowingly made wrong moves all the time. And sometimes got away with them. The question was whether this was too big a blunder? Were the stakes too high? Were his reasons too . . . too nebulous, too idiotic?

He wondered what would happen to Stefan if he stopped helping him now, made him get the drugs out of the house.

In the last few days, his left side had gone rigid three times, sort of stalling out, and he'd been unable to move for several seconds. He'd begun to think of this and related symptoms as the Tin Man effect. His meds were increasingly making his arms and head, sometimes his whole torso, move in erratic involuntary ways. A woman in the supermarket had stared at him during one of these episodes, jerking and twisting like a broken toy, and he'd felt sharply embarrassed, though he knew he had nothing to be embarrassed about. His body developed painful aches from trying to control the spasms. Recently, he'd begun to detect himself having trouble forming words, which came closer to making him crumble than anything else so far. Conversation was part of the essence of life. To lose that . . . He forcefully pushed the thought from his mind.

Life was closing in on him, and he was beginning to feel cornered. These days, he felt more and more that he'd been emotionally crippled in his youth, had been severely hobbled as he'd tried to establish a full-fledged life. *I never got down in the mulch,* he thought, reversing a phrase from a novel he admired. *I just didn't. I don't know why. I wasn't able to embrace the full joys and pains of life. Maybe it didn't have to be that way. Maybe*

I could have tried harder, should have tried harder. I don't know exactly why things turned out this way. But for whatever reason, whatever fundamental weakness of character I have, this is how things turned out.

———————

Back when Jaime lived in London, a French friend had once come with him to his *finca* for a short visit. The friend was quite taken with the villa—its position, the terrain, the view, all the elements that made it the transcendent place it was. He *got* it, the magic of the perch.

One wine-fueled evening, the lingering after dinner breathed fresh life into their conversation and opened up more interesting avenues than earlier. More truths came out.

The visitor said, "When I reach the end of my life and know I have very little quality time left, I'd like to come to a place like your home here, and bring a large batch of heroin. Spend my last weeks in a state of mental and physical bliss, with no worries about the consequences, or for that matter anything."

The guy was much too responsible and wanted too much out of life to go down such a dissolute path earlier in life.

"I sincerely believe," he went on, "that if after an honest consideration of hard truths, I conclude that my health is clearly beyond acceptable recovery, it will then be right and good to completely immerse myself in a warm bath of euphoria, and for my last days just gaze at natural beauty of the type that gives me the deepest pleasure."

Jaime said, "I'd be honored to have you use my house for such a sacred purpose."

The Frenchman died in a motorcycle accident four years later.

———————————

Stefan and Chantal quickly fell into spending most of their time together. He slept at her apartment most nights and deeply enjoyed sleeping in the same bed with her, though he didn't like being away from the gym bag. They had a natural easy rapport, and the nature of Teix in the summertime helped them quickly immerse themselves in one another. They were both independent people, but their coming together felt like the real thing, not just a passing liaison.

Chantal had a local teenage girl who helped her at the boutique, so she was able to easily free up time to be with Stefan. Most days, the two of them would walk down though the pine forest to the rocks far below Jaime's house, where they liked to swim and sunbathe. The water was crystal clear, and the high salt content of the Mediterranean made their bodies extra buoyant, made swimming less effort. About a hundred meters from shore was a sizeable rock that rose nine or ten meters out of the sea, and Stefan liked to swim out to it, climb to a high ledge and dive. He would momentarily soar through the air and knife into the cool water. It made him think of youth and the joyousness it was supposed to have. Chantal took a photo of him as he stood on the rock just before a dive, which he looked at later—his dark silhouette against the azure sky.

They smeared their bodies with clay mud made by a freshwater spring that spilled out of the rust-colored bluff behind the rocks, and sunbaked themselves until the orangey goop dried. Then dove into the cleansing sea. They played endless games of backgammon with its clicking and clacking, and Stefan regularly pronounced himself the champion, which was far from clear. A few times, they made love when no one else was around. They read books, talked about them, argued about who was right in a pitch-perfect multiyear fight between an old married couple in a Marquez book, all about whether the wife had put soap in the shower.

Occasionally, they drove to Muleta in the early evening and sat in the old town square people-watching, thought out loud to one another, got to know each other better.

Early on, she asked him, "How long are you staying?"

"I'm not sure. It's open-ended right now."

He didn't like to think about leaving. He just wanted to curl up in a ball and stay in this warm, wonderful place with this extraordinary woman.

She probed a few times to try to figure out further what the story was with him and Jaime. He sensed she could tell that he and Jaime didn't really know each other that well. He could also feel her sometimes think that he would leave before too long and wonder if that would be the end of their coming together. He very much wanted to tell her everything and came close a few times, but the possible ramifications and where they might lead overwhelmed him and made him freeze up when he thought about embarking on the strange and difficult conversation.

Part of him wanted to take her away with him, and part of him wanted to forget about leaving altogether.

They talked about him joining her on her next trip to the Far East. He could tell she'd be great to travel with—easygoing, low maintenance, accepting of the ways of the third world, knowing how to roll with the inevitable punches.

The forest they walked through to get to their swimming spot was mostly tall Mediterranean pines, with needle-laden branches that started high up the trunks and created a thick cathedral-like canopy far above. One day, they paused on a bluff about thirty meters above the sea and looked down at the crystalline blue-green water sparkling in the sun.

She said, "Look how the sunlight filtering through to the white rocks on the bottom make it look like thousands of little serpents are slithering through the water."

The offhand observation and standing there on the bluff with her, along with the natural sanctity of the forest, all stirred a remarkable feeling deep inside him, which he knew he'd never be able to capture in words.

A couple of times, he brought an old acoustic guitar from her apartment down to the rocks. Sang snatches of songs to her, surprisingly well, with feeling and spirit:

> *"I'd walk a mile for you, baby.*
> *So won't you smile for me, baby."*

"I always smile for you, baby," she responded, as one spread over her face.

He sang: "*I want to wrap my arms around my head, turn out the lights, and roll up into a ball.*"

And, "*Lay down your weary head, and let me see you sleeping.*"

He told her she had summer-colored skin.

———————

Antonio was waiting on a table of eight very proper Brits who were causing him minor stress. It was mid-evening, and *Sa Pina* was busy. Now and then, he worked as a waiter at the elegant restaurant when he wasn't getting enough private work. He'd just informed the Brits that the kitchen was out of the prawn *ceviche,* which three of them had ordered, and they hemmed and hawed about that. Before that, they called him over to correctly point out that the busboy had poured *agua sin gas* instead of *agua con gas.*

Sa Pina was in the coastal pine forest on a precipice overlooking the sea. To get there, customers had to turn off the corniche and drive down a long, winding road through the woods with villas tucked in here and there. It wasn't a restaurant people just stumbled on. It had started about thirty years earlier as a sandwich stand for people who came during the day to swim off the rocks below, up the coast from the spot where Stefan and Chantal went. Over the years, it had evolved into one of the best restaurants on the island. Antonio had swum below just the other day and stepped on a prickly sea urchin, and his foot still hurt.

The restaurant's clientele, like Antonio's private clients, were mostly very well off, if not downright rich. They were generally pleasant to deal with, although to Antonio it seemed easy to be nice when you were dining on *haute cuisine* in a setting as beautiful as *Sa Pina*. He couldn't help but wonder what it was like to be one of them, to have the money they had. The amount they spent there on dinner for four was a week's pay for him in high season, sometimes more. How was it that some people had so much money while so many others, not all that different, struggled to get by? It always puzzled him. And why was it next to impossible to get from the poor side of the gulf to the rich one?

He put on a friendly smile and brought some of the restaurant's woolen shawls to three regular customers at an outdoor table who were finding the night air chilly.

He was actually in a good mood. The cocaine from Stefan was selling at a rapid pace. He had a friend over in Palma and one in Arenal cruising the clubs and bars, selling twenty-, forty- and sixty-euro bags. Word was getting around that the coke was very good, and people were seeking out his guys. He should have cut it more, he thought for about the tenth time. He planned to get another batch from Stefan; he felt sure there was more. The explosion of business was going to make a real change in his struggling existence.

It was a bustling night at Davall. A band was playing—three youngsters and an aging artsy type with long, white hair on drums—crowded into the back corner of the terrace under the leafy overhang of a tree. The place was full, a variety of countries represented, little kids running around barefoot, adults of all ages in groups and mingling, hipster teens and twenty-somethings. Stefan, Chantal, Jaime, and Antonio sat at a table near the band. The lead singer was a skinny kid, around twenty, who Jaime had watched grow up over the years, at least during the summers; his father was a well-known English writer. The kid had long, stringy, blond hair that hung over his face, and he played guitar as well as sang. Slouched around at the front of the small stage area. The band wasn't very good, but they were having fun. The crowd enjoyed it.

When the band took a break, Stefan got up and went over to the lead singer and spoke to him. After a few moments, the kid shook the hair off his face and took a closer look at Stefan. He consulted the white-haired drummer, who still sat at the drum set, and then turned back to Stefan and nodded. Pulled his guitar strap over his head and handed his scratched-up red electric to Stefan. Then went over to join a table of kids who looked like they might be going to a moonlight rave at the town beach later on.

Stefan hung the guitar over his shoulder and spoke to the drummer, who then counted off and started a rhythm. With his back to the crowd, Stefan launched into a soulful guitar lead with a sweet, almost harsh twang. The lead unfolded, and he slowly turned to face the crowd and glanced over at his friends with a smile. After several bars of gradual build, he began to sing:

> "Wake up, momma, turn your lamp down low.
> Wake up, momma, turn your lamp down low.
> You got no nerve baby, to turn Uncle John from your door.

I woke up this morning, I had them Statesboro blues
I woke up this morning, had them Statesboro blues
Well, I looked over in the corner, and Grandpa seemed to
have them too."

The words were silly, but with the propulsion of a grinding twelve bar blues behind them, they seemed imbued with meaning. Stefan sang with a stagey growl and hammed it up a little. At one point, he mock-spanked the rounded end of the guitar in rhythm. The crowd ate it up. He settled in and played. He had presence.

Jaime, Chantal, and Antonio were quite surprised, though Jaime hid his. He remembered he was supposed to already know about this side of Stefan. They all smiled broadly and enjoyed the performance with the rest of the crowd. They felt a bit of reflected glory.

There was raucous applause and whooping at the rousing finish. After a huddle, the full band joined Stefan for another song, the lead singer shifted to keyboard, and the keyboardist took up the tambourine—a boisterous version of *Get Off of My Cloud.*

———————

One morning, a couple of weeks after Stefan jumped from the plane, he and Jaime went down to the rocks together. Jaime waded in, and to Stefan's surprise, swam lazily straight out for about a half mile and then back.

He clambered out and sat down next to Stefan on a big flat rock to recover his breath and dry off. He said, "The thing I hate about this goddamn affliction is the way it constantly rubs my face in my mortality. Human beings are the only animals who live with foreknowledge of their own death. But most people get to store that knowledge away in the back of their brain and don't have to deal with it most of the time. Me, I almost always have one sensation or another in my body that reminds me of my mortality and swamps me with sadness and fear. Except when I'm sleeping or swimming."

Later, Jaime realized he couldn't remember the last time he'd spoken as openly to another person. It was a relief. It occurred to him that maybe Stefan was becoming a friend.

CHAPTER
eight

"Jaime, hullo. It's Johnny."

"Good morning, sir. How are you?"

"Good. Listen, I'm over in Ibiza on a charter

job, and I found someone here who's interested

in your friend's goods. They'll take all of it

for one twenty, which he should definitely

agree to. Beggars can't be choosers. I can come

over to Portal Nous tomorrow afternoon,

but I have to be back here the next morning.

Have your friend meet me at Portal Nous with

the goods. I'll take him over. I want twenty-five percent for the hook-up and the transport. If he balks at that, remind him I'm providing him with extremely hard-to-find services. It's fair. I could probably gouge him for more. And would if it wasn't for you."

Jaime's left arm ached, and he shifted the phone from one ear to the other.

"When we get to Ibiza," Johnny went on, "I'll arrange a meeting off the boat. Your friend will have to handle that by himself, but the Ibiza people are businessmen, so I don't think they'll be looking for trouble. There's never any guarantees, though. Your friend will just have to take his chances. I'll be nearby so I can collect my fee. He'd be well-advised not to try and fuck with me."

Johnny paused to give Jaime a few moments to digest all this, then asked, "So, are we good?"

Jaime's thoughts raced chaotically. He pulled himself back into the conversation and said in a slightly startled tone, "Yes, absolutely. That's fantastic. That's great news, Johnny. I can't thank you enough. We'll see you in Portal Nous tomorrow afternoon."

After he hung up, Jaime stared out the window without seeing. Stefan wasn't around; he was probably at Chantal's or out with her somewhere.

My God, we're actually going to pull this off. It's going to happen. And it wasn't even all that hard. Thanks to Johnny and the fluke of me knowing him. Maybe it was too easy. Jaime's hand started to tremor. *But it seems like it's going to work out.*

I can't believe it. Stefan's going to get a fresh start. And a well-financed one at that. It's fantastic. I'm glad. I'm glad I did this.

Stefan's going to be over the moon.

Antonio was getting dressed in his apartment. His cell phone sounded with the signature music from *The Good, The Bad and The Ugly*—the soft wail of the wooden whistle followed by the haunting human trill and ominous underlying chant.

"*Muchacho*, I'm sorry, but you got a big *problema*," came the staccato Spanish from his friend, Carlos, across the island. "There are two French guys with *policía* on their way over there to find you. The French guys were asking around about the *bueno yeyo*. They roughed up a German kid I sold to, and he told them where to find me. They came with *policía*. It was *muy extraño*. The *policía* said they wouldn't arrest me if I told them where I was getting the *bueno yeyo* from. I'm sorry, *muchacho*, I had no *opción*. It's like we talked about—you can't be *estúpido*. They're on their way to Teix now. The French guys are not *regular*. And the *policía* don't seem *regular*, either. Something *muy extraño* is going on."

Antonio immediately knew what the problem had to be. It had been too good to be true, of course. A half-key of ultra-high quality coke at a dirt-cheap price, appearing out of nowhere. There was going to be more to the story. Stefan must have a whole lot more blow.

He said to Carlos in Spanish, "Listen, *no pasa nada*. You did what you had to do. I'll deal with them. I think we'll be okay, but we need to close up *la tienda* for a while. I'll talk to you *mañana*."

After he got off the phone, he thought, *What do these people want? Where I got the stuff, of course. I'll tell them without hesitation. I'm not covering for anybody on this one.*

Should he warn Stefan? Stefan was the one who put him in this goddamn situation—selling him somebody else's dope. This could really fuck him up, big time. He could go over to Palma and disappear for a while. But that would screw up all the legitimate business he'd built up around Teix, and the high season was just beginning. How long could he lay low, anyway? Besides, he didn't have what these guys were looking for, so hopefully they wouldn't care that much about him, as long as he spilled right away.

Not for the first time, he wondered where Jaime fit into all this. He'd always liked the old guy, although he could be a bit standoffish at times. Did he know Stefan was dealing? Antonio liked Stefan, too, for that matter, though of course hadn't known him long, and definitely didn't feel he owed him any particular loyalty. Antonio liked hanging out with Stefan, Chantal, and Jaime, the few times he had. They had readily accepted him as part of their group. Could he give Stefan and Jaime a heads-up without risk to himself? Maybe he could get one last batch of the magnificent blow. How much time did he have?

He exited the apartment and headed up the long steep flight of stone stairs that led to the upper part of the village, which always left him gasping for air. He went to Chantal's shop to see if whoever was there could tell him where he could find Stefan in a hurry.

———————

Stefan knew immediately he was fucked. Antonio had found him in Chantal's flat by himself, reading *The New Confessions*, which he'd found on her bookshelf. She was out food shopping at the covered market in Muleta.

Stefan listened to Antonio, then said, "Hey, man, I'm *really* sorry to have put you into the middle of all this. When they find you, don't hesitate for a second to send them my way. Tell them you just know me from Davall, that you met me there through Jaime. That should get you off the hook. Can we leave Chantal out of it?"

Antonio nodded.

"Thanks beyond belief for warning me," Stefan went on. "I know this is a mess for you, too, and you didn't have to. I appreciate it more than . . . more than I can say."

Antonio shrugged and said, "I wish you luck, man. I hope things work out for you somehow."

They clasped hands firmly, and Antonio left.

How could I have been so stupid? thought Stefan. *Selling to Antonio? I knew I shouldn't sell any of it piecemeal. I should have waited and got the most I could in one shot, then disappeared. But I let delusions of sticking around here slip into my head. Christ, I'm not a drug dealer. I don't know what the fuck I'm doing.*

And Jaime, poor guy. He helped me out and now look . . . I have to get the drugs out of his house right away. And he needs to get out of there, too. Where will he go? What are the French guys thinking? They probably think I have all the coke from the plane. Have divers gone down? I haven't seen any signs or heard anything.

It definitely won't work to just give them what I have. Christ, I don't even want the stuff anymore. But throwing it away isn't going to fix anything.

I've got to get to Jaime's right away.

He left Chantal's and walked down to the bottom of the alley where he'd parked Jaime's Honda. As he got there, a police car drove slowly by, along the narrow main street, less than ten feet from where he stood, headed for the other end of the village. In the back seat were two guys in street clothes, wearing leather blazers despite the warm weather. The one closest to him had a thin pencil mustache. Stefan felt a fresh jolt of alarm.

He stood there frozen for a several moments, then ran back up to Chantal's apartment and called Jaime on her landline.

"Listen, the guy from Paris, Felix, the guy who started me out on this whole nightmare—I just saw him here in the village in the back of a police car with another guy. They're here 'cause I sold some coke to Antonio, and his dealers in Palma drew attention. I'm sorry, I should have told you. I shouldn't have done it at all. The police with Felix and his pal must be corrupt—that's the only thing that makes sense. All of them together rousted one of Antonio's dealers, and now they're here looking for Antonio. Next, they'll be coming for me. You've got to get the drugs out of the house right away, and you need to get out of there, too."

What the hell is he saying? thought Jaime. *He sold coke to Antonio? He fucked the whole thing up? Just when it was going to all work out like a goddamn miracle. How could he be so stupid?*

"I don't suppose just giving them the drugs is going to solve the problem?" Jaime asked.

"No, they're not going to believe that's all there is, or we can't count on it, and even if they did . . . There's the police to deal with, too, though it'll be hard for them to arrest people if the plan is for Felix and his pal to wind up with the drugs. It's hard to say how it's all going to play out, but I can't believe it's going to turn out well if they find you at your house with the drugs. You got to get out of there. And the drugs. I'd come to help, but there may not be time, and Felix and his guys are between me and your house, looking for me."

Yes, thought Jaime, *I need to get out of the house. But the drugs—should I take them? I could leave the gym bag on the floor right inside the door with the door wide open. They'd still tear apart the house looking for the rest, but at least we'd have given them all Stefan has. Maybe that would placate them some.*

Will I be able to come back home? I don't see how this can work out so I'll just be able to return to my regular life. Have I really done irreparable damage to my sad little life? I knew it was possible, but . . .

What about the call from Johnny? He came through, even to my surprise. It's unbelievable, actually. And now everything's going to hell.

A powerful feeling welled up inside of Jaime. *I'm not going to let this stop me. We can still do this. Stefan can still sell the drugs and get away. All we have to do is get him and the drugs over to Johnny and the boat.*

Some kind of switch flipped inside him. It felt as if his irrationality shifted into some form of insanity, like he was losing touch with reality. He'd become completely obsessed with doing this thing, though it made no sense at all and never had. He didn't care. He wanted to do this. He was going to do it.

Besides, what other option was there? The alternatives were leaving the coke, which wouldn't fix anything, or directing the bad guys to Stefan, which he intensely didn't want to do, if it was at all possible to avoid.

All these thoughts flashed through his head in a matter of moments.

"Listen," he said tersely. "Johnny called. He lined up a deal in Ibiza. For the whole lot. You'll net ninety thousand after Johnny takes his cut. And from Ibiza, you can easily get over to mainland Spain and disappear. No one knows about Johnny. All we have to do is get you and the stuff to his boat. He'll be in Portal Nous tomorrow afternoon. You should go straight there from where you are now on the Honda. It should be able to make it there, if it makes it past the first uphill climb. I'll meet you there with the stuff."

Stefan thought frantically. He didn't want to leave Jaime on his own. Or leave him to get the drugs across the island for him. Especially not after all Jaime had already done for him. But if he tried to get to Jaime's house, it could backfire badly for both of them. Maybe things could still work out somehow. . . . They had to.

———————

Stefan had his knapsack with him that contained his passport and money, as he constantly did since his unplanned arrival on the island. He stood in Chantal's apartment and felt the warm energy. He glanced out the window at a row of cypress trees at the base of the mountain and in a disconnected way thought about how people manicure natural landscapes. Yanked himself back to the crisis at hand.

I love being here in her apartment, he thought. *It feels so goddamn good. I wish to hell I could talk to her, explain things, make her understand I'm not some horrible guy. People who aren't bad get themselves into bad situations. I've got to figure out a way to see her again. Somewhere down the road.*

He wrote a note:

Chantal,

I'm in a nightmare situation. I have to disappear right away. Spending time with you has been the best thing that's happened to me in a long, long time. I'll get in touch with you as soon as I can, and we'll see each other again if you're willing. I'm deeply sorry.

Love, Stefan

Burn this note—I'm serious. If anybody asks, tell them you and I stopped seeing each other several days ago because I was such an asshole.

He went into her bedroom, bent over her bed, and pushed his face into her pillow. Inhaled deeply and took in her scent, tried to imprint it on his memory, left the note on her bed.

He went outside and down the steep narrow alley. Pushed the Honda off its stand and started it. Drove out of the village.

CHAPTER
nine

Jaime looked for Elena and found her dusting in his study.

He said to her with forced calm, "Elena, I'm going away for a few days. If anybody asks, tell them I went to Barcelona to visit friends and wasn't sure when I'd be coming back. You should go home to Muleta right now and don't come back for a week. I'll pay you for your regular days, don't worry."

He made eye contact with her and tried

to reassure her with a smile. She was clearly confused and rattled; he could see she knew something was seriously wrong. He put his hand on her shoulder and gave a gentle squeeze.

As she got ready to leave, he went to his desk and put his various pill bottles in the messenger bag he used to carry his wallet, keys, and other items it helped to have with him. Then he walked quickly to the guest quarters and retrieved the gym bag from the locked closet. Thought once more about leaving it for Felix and the others but quickly dismissed the idea.

He got into his station wagon and drove down the hill, stopping just short of the last turn before he could be seen from the coast road. Stepped out and walked cautiously forward, looked around the bend, down the hill. A police car was parked there. He hadn't seen one there in the last few days, and the presence of one now seemed connected with the people looking for Stefan. His fear and tension, already quite high, ratcheted up a few more notches. The shrill buzzing of cicadas grated on his nerves; it was like blood rushing in his ears. He felt a large bead of sweat drop from his armpit and trickle down his side.

He was far from confident that he'd be allowed to just drive by and head on down the road without a reaction that had some teeth. And now he had the drugs in his car. If he took a chance and went ahead, got caught with the drugs, there would be no escape from a total disaster of one kind or another. If he wanted to change course, now was the time. He remembered a late night in London when he'd walked down a dark, empty street and seen a figure lurking in the shadows in front of him. He could have turned around, as he'd thought of doing, but instead he continued on and was violently mugged.

He returned to his car, turned it around with difficulty on the narrow twisting road, and drove back up to the house. Elena passed him on her Vespa, a grim expression on her face.

At the house, he went inside and pulled a medium-sized backpack out of a closet. He put in it the tightly wrapped packages of coke, the contents of his messenger bag, sunscreen, a two-liter bottle of water, and a small plastic bag of dried apricots and nuts. He pulled the backpack on, grabbed his walking stick and one of his Panama hats, and walked out the door, Headed up the trail that eventually led all the way to Fornabufar.

It would be a long, tough hike—a dozen kilometers over rough terrain—almost certainly an undertaking ill-advised for a person in his state of health. But it was a way for him and the drugs to disappear immediately. And it wasn't likely to occur to anyone that he'd just walked up into the mountains. When he got to Fornabufar, he could take a taxi to Portal Nous, or if needed, catch a bus to Palma and a taxi from there.

———————

He looked back a number of times. Relaxed somewhat when he got out of sight of the house without any sign of visitors. He settled into walking and thinking, and his breathing rate picked up quickly as the path was almost all uphill to one degree or another.

What am I doing? And why?

The main thing is I'm getting away from some serious bad guys

*and some probably corrupt police who are going to be paying
me a visit and are likely to get very unpleasant with me. I'd give
them the drugs right away, of course, and tell them Stefan was
somewhere in Teix. Wouldn't try to hold out for a moment. But
they probably think Stefan has all the cocaine and that he's trying
to rip them off. And I've let him stay at my house and keep drugs
there. Stefan'll be gone from Teix by the time they go to look for
him, and then they'll come back and focus on me again. What'll
they do? I don't know, and I don't want to know.*

*But this is about more than just getting away from danger. I'm
taking the drugs to Stefan to help him get away and start a new life.
Yes, I'm doing it more for myself than him, even though that makes
no sense. But still, I'm doing it. I know it's lunacy. Am I doing it just
for the thrill, to feel alive? If I am, it's unbelievably stupid.*

*But I can't just go back to my deadened existence. I've got to
see this thing through to the end. I know I'm acting unhinged. I'm
not being remotely rational or sensible. But I'm seventy-three
years old and have an incurable brain disease. And I feel like
I've never done anything real in my life. My sickness is gaining
momentum. I feel like I'm fading away, evaporating into thin air, if
I was ever really completely here in the first place. I don't care how
stupid this is. I'm doing it. This is my chance.*

He pictured himself standing on the dock in Portal Nous,
watching as the *Sabena* pulled out to sea with Stefan and the
drugs on board. What would he do then? His house would be
drug-free. In theory, he should be able to go back to it. There
wouldn't be any evidence of him breaking the law. It wouldn't

be that easy, though. These guys would be pissed off, very pissed off. Stefan would be gone. If he went back to the house, they'd be able to find him easily. He wouldn't be able to just slip back into his regular life. The situation would be highly unpredictable, not close to controllable. In the very least, he'd need to stay away for a healthy length of time, let the dust settle, then come back cautiously when he did.

He smiled to himself. *Maybe I should run away to Argentina and start a new life myself. I have plenty of investments in the States. I could sell the house from abroad, though I'd have to be careful.*

But he knew he'd never do anything like that. It wouldn't change things. Any real change would have had to come from within and probably would have had to happen a long time before.

The path was strewn with medium-sized stones, and he had to constantly watch where he stepped to avoid twisting an ankle. *I can't even look around and enjoy the view,* he thought with a laugh.

———————

He arrived at the top of the ridge in about an hour, breathing heavily, drenched in sweat, especially his hatband. He sat down to rest and drink some water, gulp down some pills. From there, the trail ran along the ridgetop for three or four kilometers, the most difficult stretch; it would require rock scrambling at times. Lots of uneven ground, up and down. Eventually the ridge would come to a massive plateau where the going would be easier.

After he recovered, he sat awhile longer, and took in the magnificence of being up there. The sky was a brilliant saturated blue, and there were just a few wisps of clouds. The views inspired awe, not only the western views he was used to, down to the sea far below, but also the eastern views through layers of forested mountains to the enormous plains in the distance, spreading out as far as the eye could see.

As happened sometimes when he was high up in the mountains, it struck him how wonderfully quiet it was—only when he focused on sound did he notice a low drone of cicadas and faint chirping of birds, and sonically they were so much a natural part of the place that the silence seemed complete. No sounds of man at all.

Looking out at the views, he thought, *This is where I'm from, for better or worse.* He had a sense-memory of gently squeezing Elena's shoulder before he left; her flesh had felt soft at the surface but firm underneath.

Yes, he wished he'd managed to make a life in one of the world's great cities to complement what he had here. But he hadn't managed it. He hadn't been able to figure out how the big swirls of people worked. Maybe it had been a disadvantage to be financially independent, to not have to work, not be pressured to have some kind of career.

At this point, though, his life was what it was. The cards had all been dealt, and the hands almost all been played. There wasn't a lot he could do about things anymore. Except maybe a crazy escapade like this. This silly gesture, this shout into the void. Even if it was meaningless, it had meaning for him. The truth was, he was enjoying himself.

He felt silly to think it, but he almost felt valiant.

———————

The backpack became heavy much too soon. Eight kilos, plus the other stuff, wasn't that much for a short distance, but for a dozen kilometers it was clear it was going to be a punishing burden. The sun beat down, though fortunately there were refreshing breezes this high up.

His body hurt in numerous places—knees, lower back, his shoulders where the straps rode, the bottoms of his feet. It was dreadful the way the body wore out and fell apart. He started to get palpably nervous that he'd taken on more than he could handle. If worse came to absolute worst, he supposed he could cache the packages of coke under a cairn of rocks off the path, but inside he felt a powerful resistance to that, if it was at all possible to avoid.

He came across an old stone hut used by hunters in times past. The thought of people spending nights on the mountain prompted him for the second time to calculate whether he'd be able to make Fornabufar before dark. It was two in the afternoon, and it would stay light well into the evening. He should make it with time to spare . . . if he held up.

Oddly, his tremor hadn't appeared in a while, though the left side of his body dragged like a piece of wood.

Because of his Parkinson's shuffle, he had to make an extra effort to lift his feet off the ground enough to avoid stumbling. The stones and protruding rocks on the trail didn't help. He got careless and caught his left foot on the edge of a rock. He fell forward, realizing instantly he wasn't going to be able to catch himself, and instinctively focused on how best to break his fall. He put his left arm out in front of him, palm inward, and braced for contact. The back of his arm wound up badly scraped in four places, all of which quickly began to sting. Otherwise he was unhurt. Big drops of blood trickled from one of the wounds. He sat for several minutes and staunched the flow of blood with some inadequate Band-aids he had in his wallet. He was furious with himself for his carelessness. Now was not the time.

———————————

Around the end of the third hour, he began to feel light-headed and sat down to rest for the fourth time. He took off his hat and let the air cool his scalp. The sensation of sweat drying on his skin was pleasing. He ate some dried apricots and nuts, drank some water. After a while, he felt better. But almost as soon as he started to walk again, the spacey feeling returned.

Something slipped in his head. Some sense of his regular life faded, leaving him in a state like a waking dream where his thoughts were more random than normal, less coherent.

A pain emerged in his right hip, soon accompanied by an exceedingly unpleasant tingling sensation, like electricity zinging inside his hip. The pain quickly surpassed the others. As he plodded along, it became like a jagged-edged knife digging roughly inside his joint. He tried something from a novel he'd read—visualizing a triangle in which he placed the intense pain so as to contain it.

But he found, as had the character in the book, that his mind was soon expanding the triangle in order to keep the torment inside.

As he did once in a while over the years, he directed his thoughts to a woman he'd met a long time before, back in New York when he'd lived there—Sari Volin. He mulled over his memory of her—attractive in a plain way, long, straight, brown hair, intelligent, quiet. He'd barely known her.

They met at a party at someone's Bohemian apartment in the village. It was a warm summer night, and some of the revelers climbed out a window onto the flat tar roof. He and Sari talked to one another in a room crowded with dancers and decided to escape to the roof as well. He was more than a little enamored by her, and she seemed to enjoy talking with him. Her looks were at a level where he could convince himself it wasn't completely out of the question.

They stood in front of a low parapet looking out at the cityscape—mostly pre-war buildings, not too high, with wooden water towers on roofs here and there. He allowed himself a little hope. After about a half hour, they agreed to go back inside, but as they turned to go, she inexplicably tripped and lost her balance. She fell over the parapet down ten floors to her death. Just like that. She was gone. He went into complete shock, totally confused, disoriented.

The police questioned him vigorously, trying to determine if there was more to the event, and he understood they had to do that. He was so rattled, his statements to them were only marginally coherent.

For a long time afterward, he couldn't shake the image of her at the moment when he realized she was beyond any chance of saving. Her face had turned to him, mouth open but strangely silent, and he'd uselessly reached out too late. When she was partway down, she'd begun to scream. And a moment or two later, stopped.

About a week later, he took out the shoes he'd worn that night and found tar on them from the roof. He couldn't get it all off and put them back in his closet. The next few times he took them out, the sight of the residue brought back the deeply sickening feelings of that night, and he put them away again. Eventually, he threw them out, though it seemed like a futile gesture.

Over the years, he gradually built her up in his head as maybe the one he could have truly connected with, the one with whom his life might have been different. The key premise of this fabrication was that he would have developed something special with her but had been denied by the appalling quirk of fate. Somehow, the fiction seemed plausible to him, and he was able to buy into it. It was, of course, a coping mechanism, not an effective one, and on some level he knew this. It was a hoax he perpetrated on himself, providing spurious bittersweet salve for his life situation, and he nurtured it. Every so often he would tear at his imagined wound, which he never let heal all the way, and he would feel real pain and regret and perversely, a corresponding satisfaction, similar to receiving a deserved punishment.

A cloud passed over the sun. He came to a stretch of ridge where he had to scramble up and down hillocks of rocks and boulders and use both his hands and feet. He stuck his walking stick under a strap on his backpack. The climbing and the use of all four limbs took a lot more energy than just hiking, and he could feel his muscles suck up oxygen as fast as he could breathe it in. He gasped for breath, couldn't get enough. On the downhill parts, he took his stick out and leaned heavily on it to keep from tumbling head first. For drops that were too big to step down, he had to sit and carefully lower himself feet first.

The toes of his left foot began to curl under involuntarily—the hammer-claw effect, as his Parkinson's doctor called it—and walking on the tightly curled-under toes created a whole new pain for him to deal with.

He began to wonder if he was going to make it. This was indeed no way to live.

———

As he trudged slowly along, he thought of winters on the island. His side of the mountain range had its own microclimate separate from the rest of the land. While the rest of the island had mild winters with a fair amount of clear skies and lukewarm sun, the western side of the mountains heavily clouded over for almost four months, with lots of rain and a coldness that seeped deep into the bones. Most people found it unpleasant and depressing, but for some reason he enjoyed it, especially in recent years. He had a fireplace in his *finca*, which he kept going during most of the cold wet season. And his walks in the mountains, under the brooding cloudy skies, even in the rain, were enjoyable in a different way than the other seasons. The visual beauty was very special—the cloud banks with various layers of foreboding grays, the dark ominous mountains, all so different than during the sunny times. Sometimes when he hiked during the winter, a deeply poignant, somehow satisfying sense of isolation came over him, a feeling of forlornness without bottom. He didn't know exactly what the feeling was, but found it strangely exalting, as if he stood at the prow of a boat crashing into waves, headed into a storm.

———————————

It's impossible to know when the crack in the rock first appeared. It could have been ten thousand years earlier, a hundred thousand, a million, or ten million. But over the millennia, the crack had spread, and when Jaime stepped on the edge of the rock, a sizeable chunk of it abruptly crunched, starting to give way. There was enough time for Jaime to step off the compromised piece before it fully broke off, but as he reflexively stepped toward still intact rock, the Tin Man effect kicked in, and he went rigid for a few seconds. While he was frozen, the piece gave way completely. He fell about twenty-five meters into a fissure, and a sharp edge of stone caved in the left side of his cranium.

The backpack with the coke in it was still strapped over his shoulders, a faint dusting of white powder on the outside from some of the packages bursting open on impact.

EPILOGUE

Stefan sat inside the yacht restlessly and waited for Jaime. And waited. Tense in the extreme. He'd slept on the ground the night before, hidden behind some bushes, and felt like shit. He speculated with Johnny as to what the situation might be. They tried Jaime's cell to no avail. Was he just delayed and would be there shortly? Had he encountered Felix and company? Were the drugs gone? Should Stefan leave the boat and try to find out what happened? It never crossed his mind that Jaime might have ripped him off, and Johnny rejected the thought as quickly as it occurred to him.

In the morning, Johnny said the boat had to leave—his client expected him. Stefan had to make a decision.

When the yacht pulled out, Stefan was on it, clinging to a slight vestige of hope that Jaime would somehow follow him quickly to Ibiza.

───────────

Chantal was stunned when she read the note. She could barely absorb it, didn't know what to feel. It brought home like a blow how important Stefan had become to her in their short seventeen days. The time had been so full, seemed so much longer. A despondency and resignation set in. After a time, it began to lift, but on some level she still waited and hoped.

Antonio gave her some sense of what had happened.

Both she and Antonio and the whole village were mystified as to what had become of Jaime. As was Johnny. And Elena. Rumors abounded.

Full summer arrived, and the village swelled and became ultra-vibrant for many weeks. Davall was packed most nights.

Then the high season was over, and the village returned to its remote and quiet age-old ways.

───────────

Stefan made his way to London and settled into an impoverished existence there—a city where the impoverished life was widespread and in some circles virtually an art form. He struggled to make ends meet and came to fully accept that his young carefree life was gone for good. He thought about the wonderful life Jaime had on the mountainside overlooking the Mediterranean and was baffled why he wasn't able to appreciate it. Sometimes, for fun, he imagined Jaime living in Argentina with a new life blooming, but knew it wasn't so. He thought about Chantal and contacting her. But felt bad about himself and his life. Ashamed. Sometimes thought about just getting on a plane and flying to the island, though the modest cost of the trip was more than he could afford. Of course, he thought about calling and writing, too. But held off, waited too long. The currents of life flowed on.

He daydreamed often of living with Chantal in Jaime's beautiful *finca*, the two of them happy and growing old together.

The Moment

a story

Tom Lawrence walked up the stairs of the Metro station and out into the chilly autumn air. It was late morning, a Friday. He paused on the sidewalk to get his bearings and took in the working-class neighborhood. He vaguely remembered it from a few long-past visits. The art nouveau station sign over the stairway caught his eye—green wrought iron, Porte de Clignancourt. He smiled. He'd always thought art nouveau was a bit inelegant, a bit showy, though eye-catching and having a definite appeal. Today, it looked superb without qualification.

The sky was overcast with a hint of rain in the air. There was a café next to the station entrance with a bright red awning advertising Stella Artois. At one of the outside tables, a couple of local men with jackets on sat and drank amber-colored beer and smoked fat yellowish cigarettes. A waiter came out with sandwiches balanced on a tray, pink ham sticking out the sides of sliced baguettes. Tom looked around again and sighted the beginnings of the famous flea market a block away. He headed toward it.

He was in Paris unexpectedly, and he supposed, uncharacter-istically. He'd been in London on a rare, foreign business trip—he was a corporate partner at a midsize Manhattan law firm—and the business had wrapped up sooner than expected. He'd decided to visit Paris for a few days before returning home. Being so near, relatively speaking, he'd felt a sudden urge to see the city again, walk its streets, take in its special aesthetic and sensibility. He hadn't been there in a long time—more than twenty years—much to his disappointment in himself. He was surprised at his impromptu decision, as had been his wife, Lisa, when he called to tell her, though she hadn't discouraged him.

"Oh," she said in a puzzled tone. "Well, all right, if you want to. You'll miss Jessie's soccer game this weekend . . ."

When they said their good-byes, she told him to have a good time. The spontaneity was unlike him, or at least unlike the person he'd been for the last couple of decades. He was fifty-three.

God, he thought as he walked down the street, favoring one leg slightly from a high school football injury, *what happened to me? I used to travel all the time when I was young. I just stopped.* He thought about Lisa, who'd never really been drawn to foreign travel, and their two boys, the oldest a freshman at Amherst, the younger a few years behind. He thought of their country house in the Berkshires, not used as much since they'd moved out of Manhattan to Westport. And thought about his career, which by its nature had consumed an enormous chunk of his life. All these life elements had made for a more settled existence, a less adventurous one. Typical things that happened to lots of people, features that most people wanted their lives to include. He heaved a sigh and plunged into the large, sprawling flea market.

Rows of temporary stalls enclosed in canvas or sheets of plastic, open in front. Aisles between them crowded with people. Underfoot the hard-packed dirt of vacant city lots. In one area, the stalls sold all leather jackets, with Arabs standing out front exhorting passersby. Next, Tom came on a profusion of stands selling mostly used clothing and some new——cut-rate or made by fledgling designers.

He browsed back and forth along the rows, then came out onto a blocked-off street filled with fixed wooden stalls, the countertops covered with socks and sweaters, knickknacks, used records, and assorted other items. Tending one booth was a fat, middle-aged woman with blotchy red cheeks and several missing teeth. Another booth was looked after by a scruffy youth wearing fingerless gloves. There were various food stands; Tom remembered the street food in Paris could be quite good, but he'd had a big breakfast at his hotel. He came upon a street musician, a dwarf with a hunchback who stood off to one side and played a zither, with its atmospheric ringing chords, and sang with his eyes closed and a rapturous expression on his face. A cardboard box lay at his feet, the bottom covered with coins and a few notes.

Tom plunged farther into the labyrinth, down alleyways lined with open-front stores, goods spilling outward. More clothing, lots of used furniture—plain, quasi-antiques, kitsch, all mixed together, some of it looked a bit worse for wear. One alley felt especially familiar, and he felt sure he'd walked along it on one of his long ago visits. In his late twenties and early thirties, he'd lived in London, transferred there at his own request by the Wall Street law firm he'd worked for at the time. Early on in his time there, he met a young Danish woman who lived in Paris and became his girlfriend. He often visited the beautiful city. One of his big regrets, as he'd heard other people say over the years, was that he'd never managed to live in Paris. *Eh, life,* he thought with a shrug.

He came to a more established street, narrow and lined with permanent shops. The curios and antiques in the windows were of a noticeably higher quality than the goods he'd seen in the rest of the market. In the first shop, he found a beautiful little vial, cylindrical and made of ivory, delicately carved and stained a rose color that had faded. The shopkeeper said it had been used to hold some kind of powder but wasn't sure what. Tom haggled a bit and bought it.

A few shops later, in a particularly cluttered one, he browsed in the back and carefully picked his way among the hodgepodge of objects. His eye was caught by a photograph—black and white, eight by ten, a young couple sitting on a bench embracing lazily, in a small cobblestone square with old stone houses around its periphery. The picture had a thin black wood frame, without decoration. For a moment or two, Tom thought it was merely a nice photo—something about the naturalness of the figures, the mood; he could see the sun was shining in the quiet-looking square, and the couple looked to be basking in more ways than one.

But then, he became aware of something more. His skin tingled; an eerie feeling flooded through him. The jumbled shop around him receded abruptly, leaving him and the photo in a vacuum. He picked up the framed photograph and looked at it closely, transfixed for several long moments. He couldn't believe it, wondered at the chances. It was Katja. And him. A long time ago. A different time.

Thoughts, feelings whirled inside him. He remembered exactly when the photo had been taken, remembered everything about the moment. He'd reflected on it many times afterward, though not in a long time. He pulled up memories of Katja, the two of them together, how it had been. Wondered what had become of her. She was probably in Copenhagen.

"*Aimez vous cette photo?*" The shopkeeper jarred his reverie.

"Uh, I'm sorry," Tom said, looking up.

"Do you like the photo, monsieur?" the man asked.

Tom looked back at the old black-and-white print. "Where did you get it?" he asked.

"At a warehouse for dealers."

It didn't really matter where it came from, Tom knew. It had been taken by a complete stranger who'd come and gone in a matter of moments. "How much is it?" he asked. He didn't hear what the man said but handed him a hundred-euro note.

As Tom stood at the shop's old wooden counter, its surface worn to a smooth indentation, it crossed his mind to tell the man it was him in the photo, to astonish him with the extraordinary coincidence. But he was immersed in contemplation and strange sensations and didn't want to talk about it yet, break the spell. The man handed him his change and the picture wrapped in plain cream-colored paper with a white string. Tom left.

He found his way out of the market. He wanted to sit down,

absorb the whole situation. Wanted to savor the unusual interior experience he was having, without distraction. He emerged on the street he'd come from, walked in a daze to the café he'd seen earlier, and sat down at one of the outside tables. Wasn't sure what he should order—Scotch or coffee or what? He settled on a beer.

There was something rare and special about the mood that enveloped him, disturbances reverberating within. He laid the picture on the round, Formica-topped table and undid the wrapping. Gazed at the photo, preoccupied with reflection and emotion.

He thought of the moment, the one in the photograph. And how for a long time he'd viewed it as the happiest moment in his life. Hadn't ever really stopped thinking of it that way; the poignancy had eventually just faded. He considered why he'd had that view, the ingredients that had gone into making the moment what it was—the person he'd been, his life till then, Katja, the person she'd been, and as always, circumstances. He was well aware people tended to idealize situations and events in their memories.

He played over in his head, like a slideshow, the various scenes leading up to the moment, in reverse—sitting in Katja's Montmartre apartment for the very first time, the night at Hotel Saint Simon, their dinner together in London, the magical night when he'd first seen her. And the Sunday in early March, when he hadn't even known she existed.

He'd been sitting by himself on a mostly empty beach in Barbados. It was 1986; he was twenty-nine years old. It was late morning, sunny. Seated on the sand, knees drawn up, arms resting on them, he stared sightlessly at the horizon. He felt very low. He'd just seen his quasi-girlfriend, Sheila, off at the small local airport; her flight home to New York departed much earlier in the day than his back to London. At the time, he had been living in gray, wet London for five months and was very lonely there. Not that he regretted moving; he'd intensely wanted to experience living outside the US and knew that loneliness was part of the deal, but still . . . The English were difficult, and the city was dreary in more ways than just the weather.

For immigration reasons, he'd been required to leave the UK and reenter. Complying in a rather over-the-top way, he arranged to meet Sheila in the Caribbean. He liked her and they had a pleasant time, as they always did, but toward the end of the trip, he began to feel down. He didn't love her and knew the relationship wasn't his future. Maybe more of a factor in his despondency was that he was acutely aware that Isabel, his girlfriend from law school days, supposedly the big love of his life, was getting married soon. He'd broken things off with her a couple of years back because he hadn't felt satisfied, but had never emotionally completed the split. On top of all that, as he sat there by himself on the beach, he was conscious that he wasn't about to fly home to the city he loved, New York; he was headed for his new home, where he hardly knew anybody. The long plane ride was going to depress him. He gave in to a big dose of self-pity, felt very alone in the world, and not at all positive about the state of his life. In a moment of triteness, he wondered, *What will become of me?*

Late the next afternoon, back in his office in London, jet-lagged, he called Isabel in New York. He felt a strong need to make contact with her. She answered her phone at work—a magazine—and said almost right away, "Tom, I got married this past Saturday."

He felt like he'd been punched in the stomach and was having trouble getting air. While he'd known the marriage was coming, he'd thought it was still a ways off.

"I'm sorry I didn't tell you when it was going to be, but I didn't want any last minute phone calls upsetting me."

He understood. He'd have liked to think he wouldn't have made such a call, but it wasn't completely beyond him. His eyes filled with tears; a few overflowed and trickled down his face. He and she talked in an empty way for a few minutes longer. She and her husband, who Tom knew about but had never met, were leaving in a few days for their honeymoon in Hawaii. Tom and Isabel somberly said good-bye, wisely leaving much unsaid.

That night, at his local bar in South Kensington, Tom met a young Canadian named Kathy, who lived in London. She immediately started mentioning various rock musicians in ways to suggest she knew and hung out with them. Some he'd heard of, others not. She talked in a scattered way, and between that and the name-dropping, it struck him that she had a screw or two loose. But she was pretty, and he definitely didn't have anything else going on, so when she suggested they go into the West End to grab a bite to eat, he agreed. They drove in his company car, a bottom-of-the-line BMW. He proposed a private club where they had a restaurant and he'd recently become a member—Sheila, of all people, had a connection who'd arranged membership for him.

As they entered, the first thing he noticed was a table of five exceptionally attractive people, three women and two men. One of the women in particular caught his attention. Her face had ideal northern European features, and she looked much like a young Ingrid Bergman. She was laughing at something somebody at her table had said and seemed both animated and relaxed.

Tom and Kathy were seated at a table across the room, but he was pleased to find there was a clear line of sight between him and the beautiful woman. He made conversation with Kathy and glanced across the room every so often. The wondrous woman's face had intelligence in it. And she had a graceful manner as she talked and laughed and gestured. She wore almost no make-up. A true natural beauty.

Every so often, he casually glanced across the room at her, and it felt like an hour passed before she finally met his look briefly. Then more time passed as he intermittently looked her way and she didn't look back. At last, she almost imperceptibly returned his smile. He soared inside.

As the evening progressed, they subtly flirted with one another at a distance. He became increasingly bored and annoyed with Kathy, who implied she'd recently had sex with Brian May, the guitarist from Queen. He intensely wanted to meet the beauty but couldn't see how. To just walk up to her table wasn't within the bounds of acceptable behavior. Particularly because there were guys there, though it didn't seem she was with either of them. To make his frustration worse, he felt sure she wanted to meet him, too. Eventually, though, he concluded the situation was impossible, and he couldn't tolerate Kathy any longer. With a regretful glance over his shoulder, he and Kathy left the restaurant, and he drove her to her flat in Bayswater.

After she walked away, he sat in his car with the engine idling softly and felt as he had on the beach the morning before, but with more sting.

Christ, I really wanted to meet her. And she wanted to meet me. But we just couldn't make it happen. It's goddamn ridiculous.

He'd always hated the fact that people had so little control over their lives, the way major life paths could be determined by tiny quirks of fate. Here they were, he and the woman, passing one another in a sprawling crowded city to disappear into the vastness of the planet. It killed him. He sat there, noticed it was drizzling, as it almost always seemed to be there. Then abruptly put the car in gear, made a U-turn, and raced back to the club.

She and her friends were still there, much to his relief. As before, he couldn't just walk up to her table, so he gave his card to the hostess and asked her to give it to the beauty, making clear which woman she was. He waited near the door, and when the hostess discreetly pointed him out, he smiled at the beauty and left.

Outside on the street, he felt a thousand times better. *He'd done something.* At least, he'd done something. He knew it was a long shot that she'd call, but at least he'd made it possible for them to connect. He wouldn't beat himself up for the next few days for not doing anything. He hated regret. Though later in life, he'd learn to live with it better.

She called two days later. Her name was Katja, and she was Danish, from Copenhagen, and lived in Paris.

"A dancer," she said in response to his question, in charmingly accented English. "I was classically trained when I was young. But now I perform mostly modern, and sometimes do cabaret. I'm here with a dance company I work with sometimes, to perform in a BBC television program that's being filmed."

"How long are you here for?" he asked.

"Saturday."

They went out for dinner Friday evening, and it quickly became clear his instincts had been right. She was fantastic— smart, sweet, unaffected, and every bit as gorgeous as in his first impression. And she *glowed*. Sometime in the course of the dinner, he began to fall in love.

She left the next day, but he had her phone number and address—17 rue Chappe. At their dinner, he'd said, "I'd like to come visit you in Paris. It's an easy flight."

She fiddled with her silverware. Then said, "Yes, that would be nice."

On Tuesday, he called and after they talked a little while, he said, "I was thinking of coming to Paris this Saturday, staying at a hotel. Would you be able to spend some time with me? I'd fly back on Sunday evening." It seemed to him that a short visit would lighten the pressure. They barely knew each other.

There was a silence on the line, and he felt disappointment loom, but then she said, "Yes, I'm free this weekend. I'll book a hotel for you."

Over the next few days, he was in a state of more or less constant excitement, which he couldn't have reined in if he wanted. Maybe nothing would come of the whole thing, but he had a strong feeling there was something special about meeting Katja. He hoped so.

He mulled over the recent flurry of meaningful moments in his life, each of which had submerged him in a bath of feelings, as they came and went—the morning on the beach in Barbados, the afternoon in London talking to Isabel on the phone, the evening he'd first seen Katja, their romantic dinner. The proximity of the moments, seemingly almost connected, made it seem as if there were certain preternaturally important times in a person's life, rich with possibility, the result of a confluence of events, frames of mind, and chance. It was as if the groundwork was laid by going through life, and at the key point, there was an upheaval exposing ultra-fertile ground for a brief time. He knew there were people who let these times pass by without doing anything, maybe without even being aware of them.

He also mused about the two quirks of fate that had been crucial to this possible new path—first, the initial encounter with the vapid Canadian woman combined with her suggestion that they go into the West End, and second, his access to the members club arranged by Sheila back in New York (who certainly wouldn't have been happy with the result). But for those two complete flukes, he would never have met Katja, and the door wouldn't have opened on the exhilarating new road he could vaguely see unfolding in front of him like magic.

All of it was enough to almost make him believe in fate.

Katja met him at the airport—Orly. They kissed and embraced. As they sat in the back of a taxi on their way into the

city, they held hands and talked. At one point during the ride—
he didn't remember how it came up—he told her how he'd
always felt slightly restless in his life. He thought he noticed a
hint of apprehension in her. He knew from their dinner that she
was twenty-seven, almost twenty-eight, and knew something of
men and their ways. At another point, he smiled at her and said
spontaneously, "You are absolutely wonderful."

She smiled back with pleasure, but said quietly with her
accented English, "No, you don't know. I'm a monster."

"I find that inconceivable," he said.

He'd only been in Paris twice before, but when she directed the
driver to turn off Boulevard Saint-Germain onto rue Saint Simon, he
asked with a smile of surprise, "Did you choose Hotel Saint Simon?"

"Yes," she said, taken aback but clearly pleased. "Do you know it?"

"On my last trip to Paris, I was wandering around the back
streets of the Left Bank and stumbled on it. It struck me right
away, with the ultra-picturesque street it's on, as a truly special
place. It has the feel of being in a small village, not the busy center
of Paris. At the time, I thought I should definitely stay there on my
next visit. And here I am."

In his hotel room overlooking the large garden—by this
time, he'd begun to feel as if he was in a fairy tale—they made
love for the first time. He was uncharacteristically nervous, but it
was passionate and tender, with an intensity of feeling that was
almost too much to bear.

Afterward, they went out for dinner and wound up in a touristy
place on Île Saint-Louis, but it didn't matter in the slightest where

they were, and he loved that. Two American couples sat at a table next to them, and true to form, filled the otherwise murmuring restaurant with their intrusive voices. One of the women leaned over to them and asked with a Texas drawl whether Katja was a model. Katja politely said no. Sitting on their other side was a Danish couple arguing in their own language, and Katja mischievously eavesdropped and interpreted for him in whispers. They walked back to the hotel, partly along the Seine with its row of antique street lights, and spent the night together.

In the morning, it was sunny and warm, the first really nice day of spring. He checked out, and they took a taxi to her apartment in Montmartre, near the top of one of the narrow hillside backstreets. He met her roommate, a Dutch model with bright red hair. Their apartment was small but with movie-like Parisian charm. The three of them had breakfast—coffee, juice, bread, cheese, and thinly sliced dried meat—in the living room with sunlight and breeze coming in through the open windows. Two other young women stopped by, one of them English with a baby, the other from Guadeloupe, with caramel skin. He sat there and listened as the women talked, shifting back and forth between French and English.

His inner self seemed to slip outside his body and take a position floating outside the window, looking in as his corporeal self took part in the delightful idyllic situation. *Not bad for a kid from Indiana*, he thought. He'd come a long way from his beginnings, and this situation felt like a number of the things he'd been looking for. He was in a great mood, in stark contrast to the gloomy patch a couple of weeks earlier.

Katja said, "Would you like to go for a walk around the neighborhood?"

"Yeah," he said with enthusiasm. "We're in Paris, and it's the first nice day of spring. And it's a Sunday, quiet and peaceful. Let's go outside and enjoy it." He wanted to be alone with her more.

Outdoors, it was about seventy degrees, or twenty-one as they said there. It had been a long, dark winter in London, and Katja said it had been pretty much the same in Paris. The day had a special feel, and they luxuriated in it.

"Should we go up to Sacré Coeur?" he asked, though he'd been there before.

"It will be very crowded." she said. "Let's stay in the quiet streets down here on the hillside."

She showed him her small local theater called L'Atelier, the square where her local food shops were, streets lined with especially pretty houses and apartments, some with balconies that had sprays of vines and flowers spilling out and downward. She pointed at an unusual little car parked on the street that looked like a retro-stylized toy. "That's a du-sha-vo," she said. "Whenever I think of spending time in a beach town, that's the kind of car I imagine having."

"I can totally see it," he said. "You'd look fantastic in it."

As they walked, they told each other more about themselves and their very different lives. On one tree-lined street, they heard a jumble of voices coming from behind a tall stone wall. They looked through an open gate and saw about a dozen middle-aged men, along with a couple of women, playing boules and sitting around in a small yard, part grass, part dirt, with a folding table in one corner set up as a makeshift bar.

They came to a small cobblestone square with old stone houses around it. There was a bench and they sat down. The square was on a slope, as was the bench from one end to the other, and as he sat next to her, he was slightly uphill. They were in the sun, and the sensation was like a caress. He put his sunglasses on. The square was empty and quiet.

They kept talking for a while and then lapsed into a comfortable silence. He shifted position, straddling the bench so he was facing her, one leg behind her and an arm around her. She turned toward him and they embraced and stayed that way. She felt good. Just plain good. Plus the sun and a nice drowsiness. He felt purely in love and that she was going to love him back. An acuteness of feeling surged through him that almost hurt it was so sharp. It seemed to him that this was the happiest he'd ever been, as if everything until then had been building up to this moment and here it was.

Out of one of the downhill side streets, a young man emerged and walked uphill toward them. Tom's head rested on Katja's shoulder as he held her, and he absent-mindedly watched the young man through his sunglasses. The guy had a camera slung over his shoulder and looked their way as he approached. When he was about fifteen feet away, at an angle, he smoothly dropped to one knee and brought the camera into position, pointed it toward them. He fiddled with it for an instant or two and then snapped a picture—young lovers in Paris. Like the famous Doisneau photo.

Then just as quickly, as if to minimize the intrusion, he stood and walked out of the square. Katja hadn't even been aware of it.

Tom laughed and told her. He thought how nice it would be to have a copy of the photo, a thought that would return to him over the years. At the time, though, the minor event passed, and he returned to holding Katja and basking in the sun and his happiness.

Now, here he was, twenty-four years later, staring at the photograph.

It was almost beyond belief. He couldn't fully absorb it— the picture, his coming across it, the potent swirl of memory and emotion. What was he supposed to make of it? Was there some understanding, some unique insight, he should draw from it?

Katja and he had indeed become deeply involved. For six months, they took turns travelling back and forth between London and Paris, and then she moved to London where they lived together for two years. A mighty love flowed between them. Never before or since had he experienced such clarity in terms of wanting to be with someone. But sadly, serious incompatibilities emerged, and their two strong wills clashed. After more than a year of hellish volatility, they left one another, both of them suffering in the extreme. They still loved each other, but weren't good together, and it had become clear it wasn't going to get any better. Leaving her while he was still in love with her was by far the most difficult thing he'd ever done. He moved back to New York and she to Copenhagen.

He'd sometimes thought that because it had gone wrong and hadn't lasted, his perception of the moment as his happiest was false. Certainly, he'd had true happiness since then, heartfelt but different. *My god, I have two sons I love painfully.* And Lisa, his wife, was a great woman he truly loved, though maybe she reflected the less inspired side of himself. Still, the happiness he'd felt at that moment with Katja in the square seemed like a once-in-a-lifetime experience. Vivid, palpable, filled with emotion. And the brilliant times he'd had with Katja, and their powerful love, must mean it hadn't been imaginary. It hadn't lasted, but the extraordinary moment and all he'd felt had happened.

Who knows what goes into the feelings we have? Whatever it is, we feel them, and our experience of them alone makes them real.

He sat there at the café in Clignancourt, a couple of miles from where the photo had been taken. He felt drained, numb, as if he'd just been through an intense drama, which he supposed he had. He still didn't know what to make of it, what to take away from it. Should he wonder if there was some reason he'd come across the picture? If there were preternaturally important times in one's life, were there echoes of them later on?

Did the old photo say something about his life now? Had he let himself down? Had he let his spirit go quiet, settled for an uninspired life? Was it bad that he'd stopped being restless? He thought of other lives he might have lived.

He had a flash of seeing Katja and showing her the photo-graph. It would amaze her, more than amaze her, as it had him. He thought of going back to his hotel, packing up, going to the airport, and flying to Copenhagen, just as he'd flown to Paris the day be-fore. He imagined tracking her down and her shock at recognizing him. He would talk to her, find out what had become of her, tell her what had become of him, explain the complex set of sensations the incredible photo had stirred up in him. That would certainly run wildly contrary to the staid existence he'd led for so many years. He almost started to cry, for no reason he could discern other than an overload of pathos.

He felt maudlin. He knew that some of what he was feeling was the foolishness of a man in his mid-fifties. Brought on by a mind-boggling coincidence, which just as easily could have not happened. Maybe it would have been better if it hadn't, but he didn't believe that. He felt like he'd just had an extraordinary experience, one which he would always think of as rare and special.

He thought about how things can turn out so differently than you think. Thought about the high points in a person's life, and how they can make the rest seem lesser, how maybe the high points should be kept in their place. He thought about life decisions and felt a sadness at things lost, even if for the better.

He wrapped up the photo and paid his check. Then stood to go back to his hotel and home to the life he'd chosen.

ACKNOWLEDGMENTS

In writing *Man from the Sky*, I was inspired and influenced by the fine works of many highly talented artists, mostly in very small (sometimes miniscule) ways—a term here, a detail there, an insight. I hereby acknowledge these talented artists and their fine works that are very much a part of the fabric of my life.

The artists concerned and/or their works are: Claude Klotz (for writing the film *L'Homme du Train*); Robert Stone (for his novels *Hall of Mirrors* and *Dog Soldiers*); Arturo Perez-Reverte (for his novel *Queen of the South*); Dean Wareham of Luna (for his song "Chinatown"); Matt Johnson of The The (for his song "This Is The Day"); Mike Scott of The Waterboys (for his song "Too Close to Heaven", the live recording of which is one of the most magnificent pieces of music ever created, period, the end); Tom Rush (for his song "Urge for Going"); Blind Willie McTell (for his song "Statesboro Blues"); Mike d'Abo (for his song "Handbags and Gladrags"); Robert Mckee (for an idea expressed in his book *Story*); Christopher McQuarrie (for a phrase from the film *The Usual Suspects*); and Mick Jones from Big Audio Dynamite (for the title of his song "Innocent Child"). Thank you.

For help in improving my writing and/or for believing in me when few people did, I'd like to thank Martha Hughes, Michele Orwin, Lorraine Fico-White, Sylvia Coleman, Gae Buckley, Rez Safinia, and Dean Wareham. I would also like to extend a special thanks to all the daytime staff in recent years at Soho House New York, where I wrote much of this book.

Lastly, I would give an extra special thank you for life support to Dana, Toby and Billie.

ABOUT THE AUTHOR

Danny Wynn is a full-time fiction writer, and before that, he was an executive in the record industry and part-time fiction writer. He has lived in New York City, Los Angeles and London, and now makes his home in the West Village, in Manhattan, with his wife and two children. His other favorite place in the world (after the West Village) is the island of Mallorca, Spain.

He is currently finishing two novels.

You can find out more about Danny Wynn at dannywynn.net.